MOTIVES

SECOND NOVEL IN THE CASEY RICKMAN

SERIES

KC LEWIS

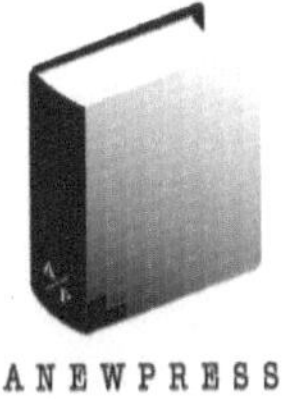

ISBN 978-1-9701-0904-7

Published April 2019

A N E W P R E S S

Table of Contents

Acknowledgements v
Chapter One 1
Chapter Two 5
Chapter Three 7
Chapter Four 11
Chapter Five 15
Chapter Six 19
Chapter Seven 23
Chapter Eight 25
Chapter Nine 27
Chapter Ten 31
Chapter Eleven 35
Chapter Twelve 41
Chapter Thirteen 43
Chapter Fourteen 47
Chapter Fifteen 51
Chapter Sixteen 55
Chapter Seventeen 57
Chapter Eighteen 59
Chapter Nineteen 67
Chapter Twenty 71
Chapter Twenty-One 73

Chapter Twenty-Two 79
Chapter Twenty-Three 81
Chapter Twenty-Four 85
Chapter Twenty-Five 91
Chapter Twenty-Six 95
Chapter Twenty-Seven 97
Chapter Twenty-Eight 99
Chapter Twenty-Nine 105
Chapter Thirty 109
Chapter Thirty-One 115
Chapter Thirty-Two 119
Chapter Thirty-Three 125
Chapter Thirty-Four 129
Chapter Thirty-Five 133
Chapter Thirty-Six 135
Chapter Thirty-Seven 137
Chapter Thirty-Eight 141
Chapter Thirty-Nine 145
Chapter Forty 151
Chapter Forty-One 155
Chapter Forty-Two 159
Chapter Forty-Three 163
Chapter Forty-Four 167
Chapter Forty-Five 169

ACKNOWLEDGEMENTS

To my family and friends for your continued support and excitement for the upcoming books.

To my husband for listening to me brainstorm out loud and giving me some ideas to make the book better.

Kayla Sullivan, Emily Conley, Krissa Lynch, Gabby Childers, Debbie Collins, Katie Somers, Siobhan Blakeney, Hailey Ford and Ms. Cheryl for the brain storming sessions, suggestions and your feedback.

Cindy Pierce for your help with the editing process.

CHAPTER ONE

"Paperwork, I hate freaking paperwork," Casey sniped as she threw the spreadsheet on the desk. She rubbed both her eyes and slid her hands through her hair fixing it into a ponytail. She used the elastic holder that was around her wrist, to keep it up.

Bernie, who could pass as her brother with the same color red hair, looked up from his work. He rubbed his newly shaved head, laughed and said, "Don't worry, Jeremy and Marissa will be back soon."

"I know ... but when is Elizabeth going to learn to keep her mouth shut? She causes way too much trouble that Marissa and Jeremy have to rescue her from; I've heard the stories." Casey paused. "I'm getting worried though, since they haven't contacted us."

"I'm sure if they were in trouble and needed us they would call; besides, we don't know if it was Elizabeth's fault. We don't know what happened."

Casey shrugged her shoulders, sighed and picked up the spreadsheet to start working again.

Casey, a witch with vampire abilities, and Bernie, a one hundred-year-old vampire, were put in charge of the vampire bar, Nocturnal; while the owners Marissa and Jeremy went to smooth things over with the vampire clan in North Carolina.

Elizabeth and Julia, both five hundred-year-old vampires, had gone down for a business merger a month earlier. They were gone almost three weeks when Jeremy received a phone call saying they were in trouble and needed help.

About an hour later, Casey had finished ordering items for the bar and balancing the books when Michael walked in the office, with two Harley Davidson bags.

Michael was five-eleven with dark brown hair, in a military cut. His mustache met with his goatee and his golden, tanned skin tone brought out his blue eyes. He was wearing a Harley Davidson t-shirt and blue jeans, that showed off all his muscles and slim waist.

Casey smiled when she saw him and her stomach fluttered.

They both had feelings for each other and knew how each other felt because of their powers but had only voiced it once.

However, it was a different story when they had first met.

Michael liked how she carried herself and didn't take any of his shit. He didn't know how to show her, so instead, he acted like a child and picked on her.

Casey gave him another chance and with everything they went through, they fell for each other.

Michael was human but had vampire abilities, which was given to him by a serum from Jeremy. He took it so he could help save Casey after she was kidnapped by the werewolves.

Casey's a witch, whose powers manifested when she was secretly being injected a serum, by Peter, the head werewolf. The serum she took from Jeremy, was made especially for her, so it wouldn't interact badly with the first serum given to her by Peter. Jeremy's serum gave her the ability to heal quicker than a human and the strength of a vampire. It also enabled her to keep the other powers that were brought out from the werewolf's serum.

Her powers mingled with Michael's and now they have a link between them, so they can hear each other's thoughts.

Casey, however, can hear other people's thoughts, along with being an empath. Her new power, which she's only had since the serum Jeremy gave her, is invisibility. She's still working on controlling that one.

Michael put the bags down and walked over to Casey, who had gotten up from the desk to check out what was in them. He blocked her view, which wasn't hard since she only came up to his chest in height and her semi-small body frame couldn't see past his broad shoulders. He picked her up in a big hug, gave her a kiss and walked her backwards, placing her on the desk.

He raised a finger to her mouth before she could speak and while walking back to the bags he said, "I know you've been busy, that you are busy, but just listen. I'm sorry I closed the link between us, I had to. You were driving me crazy with numbers flying through your head. I think you need some time away from here. Have you even been outside since you've gotten to work?"

Casey shook her head no.

"That's what I thought. I went to the new Harley Davidson store on the border of Colonial Heights and Prince George. They had a grand opening sale and I bought you some stuff. Hope you don't mind."

Casey excitedly shook her head no.

"If Bernie can do without you for a couple hours, I would like to take you for a ride on my Harley."

Bernie stood up, pushed his sleeves up on his Metallica shirt and rubbed over the sleeve of tattoos, on both arms. He was six-two and when he walked by them, they had to look up, to keep eye contact. He walked over to the desk and as he sat down said, "Take her, she's getting on my nerves bitching about paperwork. Just have her back in time to help me open the bar; in about two hours."

Casey turned around, smiled at Bernie and said, "Thanks." She hopped off the desk and walked over to Michael.

Michael moved out of the way so Casey could look through the bags.

She pulled out a light weight jacket and glasses from the first bag and a helmet from the second. She put on the jacket, grabbed the glasses and helmet and they both walked outside.

CHAPTER TWO

The beginning of the year's weather was strange, cold one week and warm another. It was a beautiful, sunny day in March, perfect for a ride.

They walked up to Michael's motorcycle. It was a 1200 Harley Davidson Sportster, with lots of chrome.

Casey noticed he added passenger foot pegs with black flames that matched the handle bars, saddle bags and a sissy bar from the last time she had seen it.

She was putting her helmet on when she heard a voice from behind.

"Ms. Rickman, we need to talk."

When Casey turned around she saw Agent Jake Ivey.

Ivey was almost six feet with jet black hair and bright baby blue eyes. He had shaved his facial hair from the last time Casey had seen him, which showed his baby face. He was the SIU agent she had been dealing with on a weekly basis, since January.

Casey rolled her eyes and asked, "What do we possibly have to talk about, Agent Ivey?"

"Sidney is still missing. Have you heard anything new about what happened to her?"

Casey laughed and said, "Well ... I haven't heard anything new since last week when you asked me. No offense, I know you're doing your job but I'm not Sidney's keeper. I don't know where she went and after what she did to us, I don't care either."

Sidney, was Casey's best friend for a year and a half, until it came out a month ago, she was an undercover agent for the Supernatural Investigations Unit. Sidney doubled-crossed everyone at Nocturnal, including Casey.

Casey had a vision of Sidney the night her betrayal came out. She had a feeling about what happened to her but wasn't going to tell Agent Ivey, anything.

"I believe you have your own opinion about what happened."

"I'm sorry, but I don't ... you have a good day, Agent Ivey."

"I'll be watching."

"Watch away, we have nothing to hide." She finished buckling her helmet, zipped up her jacket and mounted the back of the bike.

Michael started the bike and with a loud thunder, drove away from Agent Ivey. When he stopped to pull out of the parking lot he turned to Casey and said, "You're too nice to him. He already has a crush on you, don't encourage him."

"I'm not blind, I know he does but he's just doing his job. There's a saying; keep your friends close and your enemy's closer. Don't worry, I know what I'm doing."

"I hope you do."

Chapter Three

Michael pulled out onto the main road and opened the throttle to seventy miles per hour. When he stopped at the first light, he pivoted around and saw a big smile plastered on Casey's face. He yelled over the engine, "You're going to end up catching a bug if you don't close your mouth."

Casey laughed and said, "I feel like I'm flying."

The light turned green and they took off but this time Casey kept her mouth shut.

They had been riding for what Casey thought was thirty minutes when she was finally comfortable being on the bike. She relaxed and closed her eyes, just to feel the wind on her face.

A few minutes later, Michael stopped to get gas.

Casey got off the bike and stopped. She couldn't move because her ass was numb and legs were stiff.

Michael laughed at her as he was filling up the gas tank.

Once she started getting the feeling back in the lower half of her body, she walked around to loosen up. She looked at her watch and realized they had been gone for an hour and thirty minutes. She hobbled over to Michael and said, "We have to head back so I can help Bernie open the bar."

"How do you like it so far?"

"It's exhilarating! I feel so free when we're riding. Thank you ... I really needed this."

Michael gave her a hug but when he bent down to kiss her, their helmets hit and they started laughing.

He backed up and blew Casey a kiss.

She acted like she caught it and blew one back.

Once the display of affection was over, they got on the bike and headed back towards the bar.

A few miles away from their destination, she realized they were being followed by Angel and Markus.

Markus, was Casey's husband that died in a car accident the previous November. At the end of January, she found out not only was he alive, he was a werewolf and the one that had her kidnapped. While she was being held captive, he explained that his boss, Peter, had been injecting her with a serum that brought out her hidden trait for magical powers.

The serum made Casey more powerful than Peter thought it would, which was the reason for kidnapping her; to keep her out of the way.

Peter was no longer a threat because Markus killed him before he could kill or turn Casey.

The vampires and werewolves made a truce to fight against the new threat instead of against each other. They found out the new threat was a government agency called Supernatural Investigation Unit, SIU for short.

In the last month, Markus, even though he still cared for Casey, had realized that Michael was better for her and made her happy. After Markus stopped giving them a hard time and behaved himself; him and Michael became good friends.

Angel is one of the werewolves that came over with Markus and his girlfriend. Even though her and Casey had a rocky start, they've grown to be best friends. Angel helped Casey out, emotionally, when she was betrayed by Sidney.

Markus pulled up beside the motorcycle at a stop light, rolled down his window and yelled, "We'll meet you at the bar."

Michael nodded and when the light turned green they raced to the bar.

Chapter Four

Michael and Casey pulled into the parking lot and parked, followed by Markus and Angel.

Markus walked up to the motorcycle laughing and high fived Michael. His brown hair blew in the slight breeze and he had to flip his hair out of his baby blue eyes. He was taller than Michael by a couple inches but they had the same body build.

Casey climbed off the back of the motorcycle and met Angel on the walkway.

Angel was at least six feet tall with a thin frame and Casey only came to her chest. As they walked to the door she put her auburn hair in a ponytail and said, "When the cat's away the mice will play."

Casey laughed. "Not at all. Apparently, I was getting on people's nerves and needed a break from my responsibilities."

Angel chuckled and replied, "I can see that ... speaking of responsibilities, you've procrastinated long enough. I'm scheduling a training day for us tomorrow at noon."

Casey smiled and laughed. "High noon."

Angel laughed and pushed her through the door of the bar that Michael had opened for them.

Bernie was stocking the bar when everyone walked in. He didn't miss a beat putting beer in the coolers when he looked up at Casey and said, "I see you're more relaxed."

Casey sat down in front of him at the bar and replied, "I am, thank you for letting me go."

"No, thank you for going."

Everyone laughed, including Casey.

Bernie winked at Casey and continued, "Ok, this is the plan for tonight. Not supposed to be a big crowd, so we aren't opening the outside bar. We have a new girl starting tonight and should be here soon. Markus, Michael and I are going to be security. Angel and Casey, I need you two to bartend and show the new girl our ways, but if we need help, please jump in."

As Bernie finished up, the door opened and a young-looking girl walked in.

She was about five-four with blonde hair and blue streaks, that was up in a ponytail. She was wearing a black tank top and jeans that went into her boots. She looked like she was no more than one hundred pounds, soaking wet.

Casey knew instantly she was something more than human, she felt her power.

The girl saw everyone staring and excitedly said, "Hi, I'm Autumn, the new bartender."

Everyone smiled and said hi.

Bernie, as he pointed to people said, "This is Michael, Markus, Angel and Casey." As he said names they each threw a hand up.

Autumn smiled and put her stuff down on a table.

Casey walked over to her and said, "I can show you where to put your stuff."

As they walked to the bar Casey asked, "Have you ever tended bar before?"

Autumn replied, "Yes, I put myself through college bartending."

"Cool, so really you just need to see where everything is kept."

Autumn smiled and nodded her head yes.

Casey opened a cabinet, pointed to it for Autumn's stuff and said, "I'll leave you to it."

Casey walked out from behind the bar and motioned for Bernie to follow her to the office. Once inside and the door was shut, Casey asked, "Who hired her?"

Bernie replied, "I did. Why?"

"You don't feel her power?"

"I'm not like Marissa or Jeremy, I can't feel power. Who or what did I hire, Casey?"

"She's human, however, you hired a witch. Don't worry, I don't get a bad vibe but I wonder if she knows about us and the bar?"

"Keep this between us please, at least until we figure her out."

"No problem, secret is safe with me," and Casey walked out the office to go set up her station.

Angel walked over to Casey and whispered, "What's wrong with you? You're not this quiet unless somethings wrong."

Casey smiled. "I'm good, no worries."

Angel gave her a bull-shit look but dropped it when the door opened.

Casey was still looking at Angel when she said, "Welco ..." About half way through the word she looked towards the door, saw Agent Ivey and stopped talking.

"Don't worry. I'm not here on business, just dinner."

You could see the fire in Michael's eyes that Ivey had the nerve to come here. He looked at Casey and she gave him a 'don't you dare' look, so he retreated over to the pool tables with Markus.

Markus saw the look in his eyes and said, "Dude, he's not worth it. Don't give him the power to make you feel that way."

Michael mumbled something, grabbed a pool stick and started playing pool.

Meanwhile, Agent Ivey had taken a seat in the corner and the waitress that had just come on, was taking his order.

Angel and Casey were talking behind the bar and didn't realize Autumn was listening.

Angel side hugged Casey and said, "Don't be too hard on him. He's just protecting you, from yourself."

Casey gave her a mean look and asked, "What do you mean by that?"

"Ivey's done nothing but mess with you for the last month. He's inserted himself into your life and it's like you've welcomed it."

"No, I haven't! I just don't see the point in being mean. That doesn't help anyone."

Angel and Casey jumped when Autumn piped up, "Are ya'll talking about Jake Ivey? He's harmless. He was married to my sister until … well, until she passed away. In fact, Casey you resemble her."

Angel and Casey looked at her stunned, but before either of them could say anything, people started coming into the bar.

Chapter Five

The next two hours, Casey was extremely busy so she didn't see Agent Ivey watching her from the corner.

Ivey has been infatuated with Casey from the first day he saw her, when he was undercover because of the resemblance to his former wife. He wants to protect Casey from harm, like he couldn't do for his late wife. He knows he makes her mad each time he shows up, however, he can't stop himself from wanting to be in her presence.

One person had noticed Ivey and after two hours of watching him stare at his girlfriend; Michael couldn't take it anymore and stalked towards him. As he walked up, Ivey stood up.

Casey and Autumn saw what was getting ready to happen but before Michael could do anything the room froze.

Casey looked around and exclaimed, "What the hell!"

Autumn had started running over to Ivey but stopped when she heard Casey. She turned around and flicked her hands at Casey.

Casey stared at her and asked, "What are you doing? What the hell have you done?"

Autumn was surprised that Casey hadn't frozen. As she was trying to figure out what to say, someone moving caught their attention.

Ivey walked up and said, "Autumn, she didn't freeze because she's a witch, just like you. Don't you know who you're working for?"

Casey was still confused but asked, "Why aren't you frozen?"

Ivey reached up and pulled a necklace out of his shirt. It was a beautiful pendant with a red rose in the middle of it and said, "Because of this beauty. It protects the wearer from magic. I needed something after I stopped taking the cocktail from the agency."

Casey replied, "Well, that's a nifty piece of jewelry. We'll talk about the necklace later." She looked at Autumn and asked, "How long does it last?"

Autumn replied, "I don't know. I normally just do it and then get out of the situation. I've never stayed to see how long it lasts."

Casey walked around to where they were standing. "Ivey, you need to leave before Michael unfreezes."

Ivey smiled, shrugged and started walking towards the door.

After he left, Casey looked at Autumn and said, "We need to get back behind the bar and hope only Michael, noticed what happened."

Autumn agreed and just as they reached those spots, the room unfroze.

Michael stopped and looked around. He was confused because Ivey was not in front of him anymore. He turned around, looked towards Casey and threw his arms out. No one else noticed what had happened so Casey shrugged her shoulders as if to say 'what' and then helped a customer.

When the last customer left and the bar was cleaned up, Casey looked at Autumn and said, "Ok, let's talk and fill everyone in on what happened tonight."

Autumn replied, "No problem, I only knew I would be working for vampires."

"You knew vampires owned this bar?"

"Yes, that's what attracted me to it."

Casey smiled and called everyone over that wasn't already there and they sat at the bar.

Casey and Autumn told them what happened and the looks on their faces were priceless.

Michael was the first one to speak, "So, that's why Ivey was there one minute and gone the next. Why did you feel the need to protect him?"

Autumn replied, "Because he's ... was my family. He was married to my sister. He's harmless, I promise. If he's here to watch over someone, it means something bad might happen to you or to someone you love. I think he's here to protect Casey ... the resemblance to my sister is unreal. He feels guilty that he couldn't protect her, so he's trying to make up for it with you, Casey."

Michael popped off the stool. "She has two werewolves, a vampire and myself for her protection. She doesn't need anything from him."

Everyone shook their heads in agreement, except Casey.

Autumn's eyes got big and she exclaimed, "Did you say werewolves?"

Markus and Angel smiled while each of them raised a hand.

Casey replied, "I'm glad everyone thinks I need protecting, I can take care of myself. I think it's time to call it a night."

Everyone grabbed their stuff in silence and walked out the door.

Autumn said bye and drove off.

Markus and Angel got into their car, Michael on his motorcycle, Casey in her truck and they drove home.

As they were walking into the house, Markus was getting ready to say something but Angel punched his arm to stop him and they all went to their rooms.

Michael shut the door after they walked in and said, "I don't understand, why are you protecting Ivey? If you can give me one good reason not to be mad at him, then I'll stop giving him a hard time."

Casey thought for a minute. "He wants the same thing, you do. He wants me to be safe. There's something out there he feels the need to protect me from, and he's not going to tell us what it is because of the way you treat him."

Michael grumbled and walked into the bathroom.

Casey got undressed and climbed into bed.

She was asleep by the time he came back into the room.

Chapter Six

Casey woke up the next morning to Angel knocking on the door while she said, "Wake up sleepy head, time for us to train."

Casey grumbled, "I'm up, let me get dressed and I'll be out."

A few minutes later, Casey and Angel left the house for a run.

Michael got up and went into the kitchen.

Markus was making some coffee and when he saw Michael he cleared his throat and asked, "You want some?"

Michael nodded and Markus grabbed him a cup before he sat down.

After a little time passed Markus inquired, "Have you had a chance to think about what happened last night with Ivey? Casey was pretty pissed at you."

Michael took a sip of coffee and replied, "Yeah, for now I'll stop giving Ivey a hard time but if there's a chance, where I can take him down without Casey realizing it was me, then I'm going to take it."

"I hope it doesn't backfire on you."

Michael smiled and replied, "Me too."

They talked for an hour and then heard the girls in the front yard working on their fighting skills. They went outside, sat on the porch and watched Angel teach Casey some new moves.

After the physical workout, they moved to her powers so she could try to get better control over them.

Casey sat down and was instantly in Michael's thoughts, next she did Markus and then Angel.

Once she proved to Angel that power was taken care of, she tried to work on her power of invisibility, without luck. She couldn't remember what she was feeling when it happened at the bar.

Angel saw her getting frustrated and said, "Don't worry Casey, it works when you need it. Next time you'll figure out the trigger."

Casey replied, "It's the not knowing that's getting me."

"I completely understand. Let's go inside and cool off, we've worked out hard enough today."

Casey agreed and the guys followed them inside.

Markus looked at Michael, once Casey was in her room, gave him a wink and whispered, "You need to go make up."

Michael smiled and walked towards the room.

He found Casey in the bathroom and put his arms around her. He buried his face in her neck, gave her a kiss and softly said, "I'm sorry for the way I acted last night. You gave me a good reason, so I'll leave Ivey alone, for the time being." He turned Casey around to look her in the eyes and continued, "But, if he does one more thing I think is not right, he'll be dealt with."

Casey smirked and replied, "I guess that's all I can ask for. Thank you."

"No need to thank me yet. I'm sure he'll do something stupid."

Casey rolled her eyes and said, "Please don't ruin the mo ..."

Michael kissed her before she could finish her sentence. He picked her up and put her on the countertop. He moved her hair off her shoulders and lightly pulled it, so the movement pulled her head back. He kissed her on her lips again, moved down to her chin and down to her neck.

She tried to take over but he wouldn't let her.

He took off her workout top and pants. He then let her help him out of his clothes. He pulled her to the edge of the counter and she felt he was ready for her, as they kissed.

She didn't want to be teased anymore and before he could stop her, she had put his rock-hard penis in her wetness of womanhood.

They both let out a small moan and he started to quickly move in and out. Ten minutes later, at that pace, he had to stop.

She looked at him, shook her head no and continued the pumping for him.

He didn't last very long because he had wanted Casey badly, for the last couple days. He gave her another kiss and softly said, "I really am sorry for the way I acted."

Casey smiled, hopped down from the counter, took his hand and they got into the shower.

They took turns washing each other and when they were done, Casey looked at him and whispered, "I just want you to know I love you and only you." She gave him a hug and as he wrapped his arms around her, he said, "I love you too."

They left the bathroom, got dressed and when they walked out to the living room, Angel and Markus were waiting for them.

The two couples left the house in Casey's Tahoe and went to the bar.

Chapter Seven

As they were walking to the door of the bar, Markus said, "We're glad you two made up."

Casey looked at him wide eyed.

Markus continued, "Yeah sweetie, we heard."

Everyone was laughing when they walked through the door of the bar, until they saw Bernie's face.

While the others sat down Bernie started pacing and said, "I couldn't reach you. Jeremy called about thirty minutes ago, something went terribly wrong in North Carolina. He said something about SIU, werewolves, traitors, a trap and Marissa is really hurt."

Bernie saw the look on Casey's face. He stopped pacing, sat down and continued, "Just because we're vampires doesn't mean we can't die. Our injuries can be so bad that our body can't heal it, or it takes a long time to heal and we're vulnerable during that time."

"What happened to Marissa?"

"She went to talk to Alexis, their head werewolf, and they didn't see eye to eye."

"How come Jeremy didn't go with her?"

"Marissa snuck out while he was taking care of Elizabeth and Julia, who are on the verge of death.

He's been told to stay away from Lexi's Place, it's the bar owned by the werewolves in the Outer Banks, or they'll finish what they started. He needs you guys to come down to make sure nothing else happens, while they recoup. The werewolves there don't like vampires so Charlie and I are going to stay here and run the bar, with help from Autumn. It's strictly a rescue mission, that's all. Here the directions to where they're staying." He paused. "There's something else ... from the feeling I got from Jeremy, you might want to go armed and not just rely on your powers. I have something that'll help."

He got up and walked to the bar, reached over and grabbed four boxes of 9mm rounds of silver ammunition. He handed them to Casey and said, "Be careful with these, you can also hurt vampires with silver."

"I thought this was just a rescue mission?"

"This is just in case. It's better to have them and not use them, then not have them and need them."

Casey looked at the boxes and said, "Let's hope it doesn't come to this." Casey thought for a second and continued, "It's going to take us three to four hours to get there ... let's go to the house and pack some stuff, plus I need to make a phone call."

CHAPTER EIGHT

The ride was silent on the way home and once they reached the house, they went to their bedrooms to pack for the trip.

Casey went straight for the safe, keyed in the numbers and brought out four 9mm handguns.

Michael stared while Casey opened the silver ammunition box, picked up one of the guns, emptied the regular bullets and put in the silver ones. She popped the magazine in, cocked the gun to put a bullet in the chamber and then set the safety.

Casey did this with all three of the pure black 9mm Taurus's and by the time she got to the fourth, Markus walked in and said, "We're ready ... I see you kept my guns and your pimp gun."

Casey laughed. "Yeah, couldn't bring myself to get rid of any of them."

The gun that Markus referred to as a pimp gun is a PT911 Taurus. It has a pearl handle, nickel plated barrel with gold overlays on the trigger and safety button. Markus had given it to Casey for protection several years earlier and made sure she knew how to use it.

"Do you still have your small back holster that I bought you?"

Casey didn't answer but went back to the safe and pulled out a black holster. She undid her pants, pushed them down to her hips, wrapped the strap around her waist and fastened it with the holster going down the back of her pants.

When she looked up both guys were staring at her. She laughed and said, "Oh grow up! It's not like both of you haven't seen what I've got."

As Markus walked towards the door he thought, '*Wonder when she started wearing thongs?*'

Casey laughed and replied, "You owe the thongs to Michael." She still had a smile on her face as she walked over to the phone.

Casey didn't see Markus give Michael a thumb's up.

As Casey dialed a phone number, Michael packed for them both and Markus went back to the living room.

"Hey Mom … is Dad there … hey Pop, a couple of friends and I want to stay at the beach house. Is the code still the same … cool … hey Dad, I'll explain when I get back but stay clear of the beach house, please? I love you … bye."

When Casey turned around Michael asked, "Do you think it was a good idea to say that?"

"My Dad should know it may not be safe for them."

Michael nodded, she handed him a gun and he said, "I hope we don't have to use these."

"Me too but something tells me we might."

Casey put her gun in her holster and they walked out to the living room, where Markus and Angel were waiting. She handed them the other two guns and they left the house in silence, headed towards Cape Hatteras.

CHAPTER NINE

Casey looked at the clock in the car and it showed eight-thirty.

They pulled into the small town of Rodanthe, drove by the water park and the vacation resort, Camp Hatteras. As they were about to come into the town of Salvo, they took a left on MAC-OCA Drive. They followed the directions that Bernie gave them and came upon a three-story house on stilts, with an ocean view.

Jeremy had felt them coming and was hiding outside to make sure no one was following them. He was dressed in all black to help him hide because his height at six-four, made it difficult to conceal himself. He also had a black hat on to cover his light brown hair.

Casey got out and as she was opening the tailgate of the Tahoe, he stepped out of his hiding place. She was so tired from the day's events and the drive, she hadn't sensed him. She only saw a figure with piercing pale blue eyes in the darkness and screamed. In one motion, she whipped out the gun, dropped to one knee and pointed it straight at Jeremy.

The scream woke up everyone else in the car and they stumbled out of the vehicle.

She stood up and put the gun in her holster when she realized who it was and said, "Sorry Jeremy ... just a little jumpy."

Jeremy replied, "Understandable, let's get your bags and go inside. I need to tell you all what's happened."

Michael and Markus grabbed the bags out of the back of the Tahoe. They followed Jeremy and the girls up the stairs and into the house.

The first level consisted of the living room, two bedrooms and a full bath. The steps were on the far wall to the left beside one of the bedrooms.

They dropped the bags and walked upstairs to the second floor, which consisted of a bedroom, a full bath and the kitchen.

After showing them the kitchen, Jeremy turned around and said, "The girls are on the third floor. I need to tell you what happened before you see them. They'll heal but it will take time."

Jeremy pulled a chair out, sat at the table and the others followed suit.

He started explaining, "Elizabeth and Julia walked into a trap. We were told the vampires here would join forces with us, against the new threat but they wanted a meeting first to set terms. When the girls got down here, they were taken hostage by the head werewolf, Alexis. She tortured them for a several weeks, even after Marissa and myself came down; that's when we found out we were tricked. It wasn't the vampire clan we were dealing with, it was Alexis and her werewolves. When she was tired of torturing them, she gave them back to us as a warning. Alexis has been giving us the run around since she found out the new threat was the SIU. She feels, she's strong enough without help and this is her way of showing to everyone not to mess with them. We found out they're two vampires that are being held captive and Marissa was tired of the disrespect. She went after Alexis for revenge. Alexis wanted to send another message so she didn't kill Marissa, though she came close. I'm not allowed to go to Lexi's Place and I feel they might attack while we're weak. The girls aren't well enough to make the drive which is why I called you guys in for protection. We need to stay here for a couple days for more healing to occur. Once their healed enough we can leave and never look back."

Casey held up her hand and said, "Wait, not taking revenge on this chic for hurting your family, doesn't that show a sign of weakness between the supernatural?"

"You don't understand."

"Apparently, I don't!"

"Marissa and I ... Alexis was our clan's enforcer. We knew she was still down here but didn't know she had taken over the whole clan."

"Your clan is based out of Cape Hatteras!"

Jeremy nodded.

"That's where I know you two from."

"We were wondering when you were going to figure it out."

Markus, Angel and Michael looked confused, however, before they could speak Casey saw their faces and explained, "When I was younger, I use to come down here with my parents every weekend. I hung out with a few misfits; we seemed to be drawn to each other. Looking back at it now, I guess we all had something supernatural about us. Anyway, I remember one-night walking to the local game place in Buxton and I sensed someone watching my friend and me. It's the same feeling I got when I met Jeremy and Marissa. So, you knew about me back then?"

Jeremy replied, "Yes ... we knew ... we knew that when you came into your powers you would be a very powerful witch and you might help us escape. We ended up handling it ourselves but now that you're on our side and down here, maybe you can help rescue our two friends. They're the only vampires left, besides us, from our original clan. She has killed the rest."

"Damn it Jeremy, is this why you wanted us down here? Why couldn't you say that from the beginning?"

"I honestly just thought of it while you guys were on the way down."

"You better be telling the truth."

Jeremy nodded.

"We'll go check out the bar after we go see Marissa, Elizabeth and Julia. I have one question. Would I have come into my powers without the serum?"

"Yes, but it wouldn't have been so many and they would've taken longer to develop."

Casey nodded her head and since the talk was finished, they got up and walked towards the stairs.

CHAPTER TEN

The third floor consisted of a game room, two bedrooms and a full bath.

Jeremy walked towards the farthest door and when he opened it Markus, Michael, Angel and Casey couldn't believe what they saw.

Elizabeth's black hair made her look paler than usual and her laying still in the bed made her look smaller, even though she had the same build as Casey. Her injuries consisted of claw marks and scratches across her face. Some of those were healed, however, the two deepest across her chest had left blood marks through the bandages. She was wrapped with bandages around her arms but you could see the dried blood from the wounds. You could also see a tremendous number of new scars from the injuries that had already healed.

Casey looked over at Julia and noticed she had more unhealed injuries than Elizabeth. Her guess was Julia took the brunt of the punishment to protect Elizabeth and her smart-ass mouth.

Julia's blonde hair was covered with dried blood and she looked stockier than normal because of the bandages. Her right arm was wrapped and set to her chest, which is what they do for a shoulder injury. Both of her eyes were all the colors of the rainbow and one was swollen shut. Her lip had been split but some healing had occurred. She had several deep cuts on her chest and left leg, however, it was her right leg that was the worst. If the damage was bad enough she would have a limp, even after she was healed.

When Casey scanned from Julia to Marissa, she gasped in horror.

Marissa's injuries were obviously done to make a gut-wrenching point, her blonde hair was stained red from all the blood. Her eyes were black and both swollen shut. Her nose was split over the bridge and her left cheekbone was broken in three different places. Her lip was split in several places and a gash down to the bone, on her right cheek. There were human teeth marks on both sides of her neck and claw marks on her chest. Both of her arms were wrapped in the position of shoulder injury with blood stains coming through the bandages from other injuries and her hips were dislocated and broken. Her injuries were consistent with someone pulling her arms, while someone else was pulling her legs, until they heard a pop.

Their injuries were so bad, their bodies had shut down and put them into a deep sleep. It wasn't a coma but close to it and they had IV's of blood pumping into them.

She could only imagine the severity of their injuries if they still looked like this now, even with some healing having occurred.

Casey realized she was standing alone. When she turned around and looked out into the game room, Markus was consoling Angel; who was crying so heavily, she ended up passing out.

Casey walked out of the room slowly in disbelief of what she saw. She couldn't believe someone would take pleasure in doing something like this to another being. She walked downstairs, in a trance, to the second floor and then to the first.

Michael followed her to make sure she was ok and didn't try to do anything drastic, like going to the bar and confronting Alexis by herself.

Casey was halfway out the front door when she came to her senses. She realized she didn't know where the bar was, so she turned around, collapsed on the floor and started crying.

Michael walked over, sat down, leaned her against him and just let her cry in silence.

A few minutes later, she started to calm down; just in time because everyone else was coming downstairs.

Michael helped her up and sat her on the couch before the others could see what was happening.

Casey got her wits about her and when everyone sat down she said, "Here's my plan. First, I want someone to take some of my blood and split it between Marissa, Elizabeth and Julia. Fresh blood is better than bagged blood and my powers could probably speed up the healing process. As for the bar; Angel and Markus will go in first. They'll keep the werewolves scent busy which will buy me some time to read people, once Michael and I come in."

Jeremy asked, "Casey, are you sure you want to do this?"

Casey started to tear up again but pushed it down and said, "Damn straight! Alexis doesn't deserve to live because of what she did to those three upstairs. It's ten-thirty now, let's get to the bar before I change my mind about not killing her tonight."

After Jeremy took some of her blood, Casey got up and started towards the door. She stopped, looked at Jeremy and asked, "Are they going to become part werewolf? How does that work and what do we need to watch out for?"

"Vampires can't be turned into werewolves and werewolves can't be turned into vampires. If the wolves are in human form, you're fine, but as soon as they turn into wolf form that's when a human can get infected. I don't know if you and Michael could be turned, you both took serum that gave you vampire abilities. Technically, you both are still human, so be careful."

Chapter Eleven

Casey read over the directions Jeremy had given to her before they left the driveway.

They took a left on the main road, went about a mile and took a right onto a dirt road by Dairy Queen.

The sign beside the road simply read Lexi's Place in dark letters. Trees lined both sides of the road and made it narrow. When they pulled into a clearing, they saw a parking lot and a two-story building. The sign to the bar was a full moon with Lexi's Place in the middle, in dark blue letters. Simple, yet eerie.

The bar wasn't packed but was doing well for off season.

They noticed while finding a parking spot there were a lot of out of town vehicles. As they parked, Angel asked, "I wonder why this bar doesn't have flashy lights, like ours?"

Casey answered, "It's a small town, no need for flashy. Looks like Alexis just wants to attract humans to the bar, without attracting other super naturals and attention to herself or her clan."

Angel shrugged as her and Markus got out of the car and walked into the bar.

Casey and Michael got out of the car and started walking towards the door. They both took a deep breath before Michael opened it and walked in. They headed down a ramp and stopped to take the bar all in.

To the left of the ramp was a long bar with a door behind it, marked office. To the right of the ramp was a staircase leading to the second floor, a large dance floor that led to a stage and booths lining the walls around the dance floor, on both sides. There was another staircase that went to the second floor, by the stage, on the opposite wall.

Casey and Michael saw Angel and Markus had chosen the middle booth farthest from the door, by the dance floor. Michael took Casey's hand and led her upstairs, which only consisted of tables and chairs, all the way around.

They sat at the table across from Angel and Markus so they could watch the whole bar.

No one paid attention to them, except the waitress. She saw them sit down and came over to get their order.

They ordered drinks because they didn't know how long they would be there. They were watching the waitress walk to the bar, when a guy and a girl came out from the door behind the bar.

The guy was about five-eight with dirty blonde hair. He had on a black button-down shirt, black slacks and a pink tie, not only to add color but to match the girl he was standing beside. He was broad in the shoulders and had a small stomach but was very attractive and looked familiar to Casey.

The girl was Casey's height with brown curly hair and carried herself with arrogance. Her pink dress came to an inch above her knees and had a low v-cut top. She was a small framed woman with an attitude.

The waitress pointed up to where Michael and Casey were, in addition to where Angel and Markus were sitting.

The guy and the girl nodded, walked over and up the stairs towards them.

Casey and Michael didn't see them coming because they were trying to get Angel and Markus's attention.

Angel and Markus saw them because they could feel the power surge from them both, which caught their undivided attention.

Casey didn't feel the power until they were at the top of the stairs. She tensed up and thought, '*Michael someone very powerful is coming.*'

Michael couldn't feel what she was feeling but put her hand in his, '*It's ok Casey, we can do this, put your game face on.*'

Casey smiled and patted his hand, '*You're right.*' She took a deep breath and let it out slowly, by the time the couple had made it to their table.

Casey and Michael looked up and it was Casey who said, "No way, Xander! It's been a long time."

Xander replied, "Yes, it has Casey. I would like for you to meet my business partner, Alexis."

"It's nice to meet you."

Alexis just nodded, whispered something to Xander and then walked back downstairs.

Casey looked back at Xander and said, "This is my boyfriend Michael."

Both guys nodded and shook hands.

Casey continued, "What have you been up too?"

"I'm manager of this lovely establishment, for the owner Alexis. How long are you in town?"

"Just for a couple days."

Before they could talk anymore, the waitress came up, dropped off their drinks, said something to Xander and walked away. He turned back to Casey and said, "Stop by before you leave, so we can catch up."

"Definitely."

Xander walked back downstairs and sat in the corner by the stage with Alexis; to eat their dinner the waitress had brought them.

Casey decided to listen in on their conversation. She realized from being around them, werewolves speak what they think. She just needed to focus and open her mind to hear them.

Alexis started off by saying, "I don't like leaving Jeremy and the girls alive. They don't have followers, nobody will miss them. I want to attack in the morning, while they're asleep."

Xander hesitantly said, "If that's what you want to do."

"You're my first lieutenant, don't second guess me."

"Forgive me, I wasn't trying to second guess you. I just thought since they don't have followers, they're not really a threat and we can leave them be."

"We could, but what's the fun in that? Decision has been made, we go in the morning. As for Casey, how much do you know about her?"

"Casey and her family use to come down here on the weekends and we use to hang out. Why?"

"When I walked up to the table, I sensed some type of power coming from one of them, which is weird because they're both human."

"If you want I'll keep an eye on them."

"No, let's deal with Jeremy first. Go and get the others ready, we attack in the morning."

Xander got up from the table and walked into the office thinking, *'She can ask all she wants about Casey. I'm not putting Casey and her friend in danger, she was too good of a friend to me when I needed one.'*

Casey was pleased that Xander felt that way after all these years and that she stayed calm, when she heard what Alexis planned on doing. She looked at Michael and simply said, "We've got to go, I'll explain everything in the car." As they left the bar Angel and Markus got up a few minutes later and followed them out.

Luckily nobody noticed, they somewhat, left together and Casey explained what she had heard, once they got into the car.

Chapter Twelve

When they got back to the house everyone ran up to the third floor.

Casey explained to Jeremy what was going on and asked, "Can the girls be moved?"

Jeremy sat down with a lost look on his face and replied, "There doing a little better, maybe they can be on the road for an hour. I don't understand why Alexis wants to finish the job. I'm sure everyone has gotten her message. We definitely have!"

Casey had never seen Jeremy lose it like this.

Alexis had broken him with the injuries she had inflicted on the girls, especially Marissa, the love of his eternal life.

Casey sat down beside him and put her hand on top of his. "She's a sadistic bitch. I'll do everything in my power to keep ya'll safe, while the girls are healing."

Jeremy smiled and hugged Casey.

This took Casey by surprise but she hugged him back.

After they released, she continued, "My plan is to move all of us down to my parent's place in Buxton. We'll be far enough away that she shouldn't be able to sense us. I'm still new to this, Jeremy, ya'll can survive if you're not in direct sunlight, right?"

Jeremy nodded.

"Okie dokie, here's the plan. Guys get the girls into the cars while Angel and I pack their stuff."

Everyone went their own way and within an hour, at the most, the cars were packed with everything and everyone.

They left the house in Rodanthe with Casey leading the way and headed south.

Twenty minutes later they arrived in Buxton and turned down Old Buxton Backroad, headed towards Cape Woods Campground.

CHAPTER THIRTEEN

When they pulled up in front of the trailer, Casey and Markus got out to see if they could sense anything or anyone.

It was clear, so Casey walked to the shed to get the extra key. She saw her Dad still had the combination lock on the door so she called Markus over.

She pointed to the lock, he laughed and said, "Some things haven't changed."

Casey smacked his shoulder, as she said, "Shut up, you know I've never been good at getting those open."

Markus smiled as he unlatched the lock and she reached in to grab the key.

Once the door was unlocked to the trailer, Casey held it open for Angel who carried Elizabeth, Michael who carried Julia and Jeremy who carried Marissa.

Casey motioned for them to go through the living room and kitchen, to the master bedroom and then she went outside to help Markus with the bags.

Walking towards the car she looked up. She was always amazed at how bright the stars were, no matter how long she had been coming down to the Outer Banks.

She stood there looking up at the sky reminiscing about past times, so when Markus came up and spoke, it startled her.

"Do you remember when we came down here for our honeymoon?"

Casey nodded her head and he continued, "That was an awesome week. It was much simpler times for us."

Casey looked at him with a tear in her eye and smiled. "Yes, yes it was."

Markus put the bags down, turned Casey to him and wrapped his arms around her.

She followed suit and put her arms around his waist, her head on his chest and started to quietly cry.

He squeezed her tight and softly said, "I'm sorry Casey ... I'm sorry you were brought into this world." Markus released his grip a little when Casey moved to look up at him and he continued, "I'm sorry for the way I treated you in our marriage. I'm sorry for everything."

Casey smiled and replied, "I know you are Markus. Your actions have shown that the last couple months. It's nice to hear it, though."

Markus moved a piece of hair from Casey's face and kissed her on her forehead. He gave her one more squeeze and let her go from the hug.

They both grabbed bags and started walking towards the door.

Markus blurted out, "I love you ..."

Casey stopped and looked at him.

He blushed and quickly said, "I mean, I will always love you."

Casey smirked and replied, "That's one thing we still have in common."

They leaned over and gave each other a kiss on the cheek, about the time Michael came outside.

Michael chuckled and said, "So, that's why the bags haven't made it in yet, you two are making out."

Casey and Markus busted out laughing.

Michael stood there with a big smile on his face, until Casey threw a bag at him. It caught him off guard and made him stumble backwards and fall. As he was getting up, he smiled again and swatted her butt when she walked inside.

She turned her head and blew him a kiss.

Michael put the bag inside and turned around in enough time to catch the bag Markus was throwing at him. He put it inside, by the other one and walked back to the car with Markus.

They were quiet taking the rest of the bags out of the vehicles and as they headed for the door, Michael said, "Thank you."

Markus smiled and said, "For what? Kissing your girlfriend, anytime."

Michael chuckled. "I was listening. I know you two have more history together, but I can tell you that meant a lot to Casey. Sometimes, you just need to hear the words."

As they were walking into the house with the rest of the bags Markus said, "I know, I also should have said it sooner."

Markus was the last to enter so he locked up.

Jeremy and the girls were settled in the master bedroom sleeping.

Casey and Angel were finishing up fixing the windows to keep the sun out when it came up. They had covered the master bedroom, living room and kitchen windows. When they finished and they all four sat on the couch, in exhaustion.

Chapter Fourteen

No one realized they had fallen asleep or it was the next day, until Casey's phone rang.

She jumped up and answered, "Hello ... good afternoon to you to Daddy ... yes sir, we made it down safe ... I'm sorry I didn't call ... yes sir, I'll let you know when we leave ... love you to."

Casey put her phone down, saw everyone was still sleeping and checked on Jeremy and the girls. Once she saw they were fine, she went into the kitchen to make some coffee. She made her a cup, once it was done brewing and quietly went out the front door to sit on the deck.

Casey had forgotten how quiet things were down here. She heard some birds chirping and leaves blowing with an occasional car going by. She sat in the afternoon sun, sipping her coffee and taking a break from life, just enjoying nature.

About an hour later, Angel came outside and sat down. She held up her cup and said, "Thanks for making a pot."

Casey replied, "We've lived together long enough to know, we all need coffee to wake up."

They both smiled.

Angel asked, "So, what's the plan?"

Casey thought for a second. "Figured we would stay here until the girls can travel. We just need to keep a low profile, so Alexis won't link us to Jeremy."

"I agree. Hey, do you think Jeremy would give us some time off? Maybe we can stay down here for a couple days, after they go back. I think we've earned a vacation."

"I don't know if that would be a good idea or not, with Alexis down here."

"If she doesn't figure out that we're with Jeremy, we should be fine."

"We'll see, depends on if Jeremy lets us off."

They sat back and enjoyed the sun in their faces and were woken by Michael. "Casey, Angel come inside, there's something you need to see."

Once inside, Casey grabbed her phone and checked the time. It was five o'clock.

Jeremy walked out of the bedroom as she put down her phone and said, "I want to say thank you so much for giving your blood to them. I didn't foresee it helping this much." As he finished his sentence, Elizabeth walked out of the room.

What was left of her injuries were shallow cuts on her arms. To her dismay, everyone hugged her and Angel helped her to the couch.

Casey squeaked in excitement when Julia came out of the bedroom.

Julia's bruises were gone from her face, her eyes were open and her shoulder was healed from the injury. Her other injuries were healed too, except her right leg; she was walking with a limp.

Casey turned around from helping her to the couch and saw Marissa, standing at the edge of the kitchen.

Everyone's jaw dropped.

Marissa's face was completely healed except for where the gash on her right cheekbone use to be, there was a shallow cut. The teeth marks were gone and the claw marks were shallow cuts as well. Her arms and shoulders were also completely healed and although she was walking, she was moving slow.

Marissa smiled at Casey and maneuvered her way to her, picked up her hand and said, "Thank you so much for trying something new. We would've never thought to use your blood. I ... we owe you."

Casey had tears coming down her cheeks and Marissa wiped them away.

Casey replied, "You guys are most definitely welcome. Ya'll mean a lot to me."

Jeremy walked up and him and Marissa gave Casey a hug at the same time. When they had collected themselves from being emotional, Jeremy and Marissa stepped back.

Casey went over to Michael and he put his arm around her for support.

Jeremy looked around, laughed and said, "Look at us. We're some motley crew, huh?"

Everyone chuckled.

Jeremy continued, "Since they're mostly healed, we're not going to press our luck. We're going home tonight." He paused. "It's obvious Alexis hasn't found out you guys were with us, she would've attacked by now. I'm thinking, that you four should stay down here and have a small vacation."

Angel was very excited while Casey gave him an inquisitive look.

Jeremy smirked and replied, "I happened to overhear a certain conversation. Angel is right, you four have earned it. Take a few days and enjoy yourselves."

Casey sighed, pointed at Angel and said, "Like I have a choice, she's going to make me. Well, if ya'll are leaving let's get you packed and on the road, so we can start our fun."

Jeremy went in the bedroom and grabbed the bags. "No need, already done."

Everyone walked outside and helped get the girls and bags in the car.

Jeremy got in the driver seat and rolled the window down.

Casey walked up and said, "Send a text when ya'll get home. Us having fun, depends on it."

Jeremy smiled and replied, "Yes ma'am, I sure will." Jeremy rolled the window up and drove off, towards home.

They watched until the car was out of sight and they all turned to look at each other.

Angel excitedly asked, "What are we going to do tonight?"

Chapter Fifteen

After an hour of Casey explaining what there was to do around the island, they decided to go out for dinner and drinks.

Another hour later, everyone had taken showers and were walking out into the living room.

No one had packed going out clothes, so they were dressed in jeans and t-shirts.

They got into the Tahoe and Casey drove to the Captain's Table, for a seafood dinner.

At dinner, no one talked, they were too busy checking their messages and emails, waiting to hear something from Jeremy.

Half way through dinner Casey's phone went off. She looked at it and said, "Happy to report, they've made it home safe."

Everyone smiled and sighed with relief, put their phones down and started enjoying themselves.

As they were waiting for the waitress to come back with Casey's card, from paying the bill, her phone went off again. She looked at it and chuckled.

When she looked up, they all were giving her a 'what' look.

Casey read the text out loud, "Hey, this is Xander. I got your number from your Dad. Surprised he still knew who I was, anyways just wanted to invite you and your friends to the bar tonight. I'm the only manager here, so it would be easy to give you free drinks. Hope to see ya." She looked up at everyone when she finished reading.

Angel and Markus shrugged.

Michael simply said, "It's up to you."

Casey smiled and replied, "Well, we did all agree to make it an early night. So, since he's the only manager there, I say we go and check it out. If we aren't having fun or don't like the company, we can always leave earlier."

The waitress came back with her card, while she was texting Xander 'on the way' and then they left the restaurant, headed to Rodanthe.

They pulled up to a sea of cars and trucks because Lexi's Place was packed. They walked in and Xander met them at the ramp.

He gave Casey a hug and shook everyone else's hand and showed them to a table, that was reserved.

He smiled at Casey and said, "I was hoping ya'll would come tonight."

Casey smiled back and asked, "How did you know we were all friends?"

Xander replied, "I have people down in Buxton and they told me you showed up at your Mom and Dad's place with a few people. I remembered the other night when you and Michael came in, there was a new shifter couple that visited too. I thought it was suspicious when ya'll came and left within minutes of each other and that's when I realized ya'll were together."

Casey got nervous and it must have showed on her face because Xander quickly said, "Don't worry, your secret is safe with me. I didn't agree with what she did to them. The fact she didn't show up down there, should show you can still trust me."

Casey relaxed and replied, "Thank you, Xander. That means a lot to me."

Xander smiled, waved a waitress over and said, "Their drinks are on the house tonight, take good care of them." He looked at Casey and said, "I have to work now, we'll catch up later."

Casey nodded her head yes and he walked back to the bar.

They ordered their drinks and relaxed in the booth listening to the band. They had fun the next couple hours, dancing, drinking and just talking about anything and everything.

Xander walked over and said, "Having fun I see."

Everyone said, "Yes."

Xander continued, "Casey, Alexis came in the back door and I didn't know she's been here for the last hour. She would like to talk to you and your friends."

Casey asked, "Do you know about what?"

Xander replied, "No, I don't. You don't have to, if you don't want to."

Casey motioned for Michael to get up as she said, "Don't want her mad at you. Can't be anything too serious."

Michael gave her a look but she still got up and started following Xander.

Casey was feeling good after consuming drinks for the last couple hours. She didn't think anything of Alexis wanting to talk to them.

CHAPTER SIXTEEN

Xander took them through the door behind the bar.

The office was painted a pale blue and had pictures of different places, in the Outer Banks. There was a black couch in front of a desk, which was where Alexis was sitting.

Alexis smiled, pointed to the couch and said, "Thank you for coming to talk to me."

As they were sitting down, Casey replied, "No problem."

"I would like to start by saying I'm sorry about my rudeness a couple days ago. I was dealing with something personal and it wasn't going my way."

"No worries, apology accepted."

"Wonderful, now for the main reason I asked to speak with you. I have done some digging within the last day, about you four. I haven't found out much but what I have is quite interesting."

She looked at Markus and Angel and said, "I know you two are very new at being wolves and I can help with that. In fact, it would be, I help you if you help me kind of thing."

Casey shuffled in her seat.

Alexis looked at her and said, "I was sensing some type of power ... figured out it was you, but I can't put my finger on it, because you seem human." She looked at Michael and continued, "I've heard you're special but can't sense anything about you either, except your humanity." She paused for dramatic effect but before anyone could speak she continued, "I would like your help in finding some people and bringing them back to me. I would also like for you four to join my clan down here. What do you think of that, Casey?"

Casey was sobering up because of what Alexis had said. After a moment of silence, she answered, "We appreciate the offer, however, we have to decline. We're not bounty hunters and we try to live as normal as possible."

Alexis gritted her teeth but smiled and asked, "Is there anything I can do or say to change your mind?"

Casey smiled, got up, and everyone else got up too as she said, "No ma'am, sorry we can't help."

Alexis got up and walked them to the door saying, "It's ok, I'll find another way to fix my problem."

Casey said bye to Xander and then walked out to the car, with everyone else.

After Casey left the office, Xander turned to Alexis and asked, "What are you planning?"

Alexis smirked and replied, "Nothing." As she was shutting the door in his face, he yelled over the music, "Casey's my friend and I don't want her hurt."

When the door was completely closed and she was walking back to her desk, the phone rang.

Chapter Seventeen

Michael drove back to the trailer because even though Casey was sobering up, she was still tipsy.

Once they made it out of Salvo, Casey panicked, "That was too easy, we need to leave tonight. We'll clean up and then go."

Michael stepped on the gas and when they got back to the trailer they started cleaning.

After thirty minutes, the trailer was how they found it and Michael went to throw the trash in the dumpster.

Casey was going around making sure everything was right when she realized Michael wasn't back yet. She went outside, looked around and saw the trash bag in front of the bin. She ran back inside and yelled, "Michaels gone!"

Angel and Markus ran into the living room.

Casey was pacing back and forth. "I bet Alexis took him. I knew it was too easy, I'm going to kill her."

Angel started to say something and Casey interrupted, "Don't try and stop me. I would help you if it was Markus."

Angel shrugged, sat down and replied, "I just thought you could use your power to hear his thoughts or to sense where he is. That's what we've been working on, in training."

Casey sighed and replied, "I've never tried when someone wasn't in the same room with me."

Markus and Angel smiled at her and Angel said, "You can do it Casey, just concentrate."

Casey sat on the floor in Indian style and closed her eyes. At first, she couldn't sense anything. She calmed her breathing by taking slow breaths and started again. This time she felt his presence and then sensed his fear and pain.

A voice popped in her head, it was Michael, '*I can feel you Casey. Alexis has taken me and brought me back to the bar. Xander won't let her hurt me anymore than her guys already have and he's taken a couple hits because of it. She's using me as bait to get to you. I know I can't stop you so please, be careful.*'

As quick as the voice popped in her head it was gone.

Casey's eyes popped open and she said, "I know where he is."

Chapter Eighteen

Angel, Markus and Casey pulled up to the bar. It was three in the morning and the bar was closed.

There was no reason for them to sneak in because Alexis would sense her power. They decided to walk in, even though they knew it was a trap.

When Casey grabbed the door handle, she saw some, of what was going to happen after they entered the bar. She turned to Angel and Markus and said, "No time to explain, just follow my lead." She flung the door open and they walked in.

Michael was tied with ropes to a chair, half beaten on the dance floor with Xander standing by him, protecting him.

Alexis and her goons were standing at the bar.

When Michael looked up and Casey saw the extent of damage done to his face, she cringed.

He had two black eyes, cuts on his face and a whelp under his right eye.

Casey ran over to untie him but Alexis appeared in front of her and Michael, before she could start. Her heart skipped a beat and fear fluttered through her body.

Alexis laughed and replied, "I love the smell of fear. Now, I'll let you and your friends go, if you do the favor I asked of you earlier tonight."

Casey stood up and with a firm voice said, "We're not bounty hunters."

Alexis was pissed that Casey still said no and yelled, "Don't you mean, you don't want to turn in your bosses. I received a phone call after you left … imagine my surprise when I found out, you work for Jeremy and Marissa. I had to retaliate which is why I took Michael. Since you're here now, are you going to help me?"

Casey knew she was getting to Alexis so she chuckled and calmly said, "No, I won't help a spoiled rotten bitch. I'll take my chances with the consequences."

Xander walked up shaking his head with his black eye and cut on his cheek, that had almost healed. He held Alexis by the shoulder, while saying, "Same ole, Casey. Please stop, so you don't make things worse?"

"Can't do that Xander, you know me, can't keep my mouth shut." Casey looked back at Alexis and said, "You've already done enough damage to Julia, Elizabeth and Marissa. They won't come back, neither will we for that matter. Let Michael go and we'll leave."

Alexis gritted her teeth and tried to be calm when she said, "Here's the deal, you give us Jeremy, Marissa and the other two and then you can have Michael."

"You don't seem to understand, we're not giving up our bosses to a sadistic bitch!"

Michael yelled, "Casey!"

"It's ok Michael."

They shared a look, Michael nodded his head and when Casey stood up she said, "She thinks I'm a mere human with something special about me because she can't sense my true power source." She turned, looked at Alexis and continued, "How about this proposition, you let Michael go, along with safe passage for us ... o ... and the two other vampires you have as slaves?"

Alexis laughed while she asked, "Why in the hell would I do that?"

"Because if you don't, I'll be forced to kill you."

Alexis laughed even harder and replied, "I'm tired of this shit," and lunged for Casey.

In midair, Alexis was tackled by Angel and they flew towards the stage fighting. They rolled around on the floor punching and scratching each other. When the fight was finished, Angel was lying on the floor gasping for breath.

Casey made her way over to them and as Alexis was going to give the finishing blow, she grabbed her arm.

Alexis spun around and tried to hit Casey with her other hand but Casey caught it, before she could connect.

They were the same height and were eye to eye when Alexis pulled away from Casey and exclaimed, "Your eyes! What the hell are you?"

Casey laughed. "Wouldn't you like to know. Markus come over here and make sure Angel is ok."

Markus did what Casey asked and she stood in between them and Alexis.

After a bit of staring between Alexis and Casey, Markus broke their concentration by saying, "A few broken bones but she's going to be fine."

Alexis walked back to the bar cackling. "Pity." She turned around and looked at Casey and said, "I have a new proposition for you. How about we have a pack challenge? If you win, you get to take your friend's home with safe passage and oh hell, I'll let you take the other two vampires, there nasty creatures anyway. But if I win, I get you. Well, what's left of you and your friends can go home. That's the deal, take it or leave it."

Casey shrugged her shoulders and replied, "Deal but what's a pack challenge?"

Xander responded, "Casey don't do it, it's a fight to the death."

Alexis exclaimed, "She agreed, can't take it back now. Besides, I want to keep her so I won't kill her, however, it will take her a long time to heal when I'm done."

Casey looked at Markus and Michael and said, "This is the only way of getting ya'll out of here alive."

Markus replied, "You honestly think she'll keep her word and let us go."

Casey said, "I can win Markus, don't worry."

Alexis laughed and growled, "So sure of yourself."

Casey looked back at Alexis and said, "Win or lose my friends get to leave. I know they can handle themselves and you don't know where the others are, so I think that's a fair deal."

Alexis smirked, shook her head yes and lunged at Casey.

Casey sidestepped, went invisible and the look on Alexis's face was priceless. Casey couldn't help but laugh.

Alexis swung around towards the sound and missed.

Casey punched Alexis in the face and she went flying. She ran over to where Alexis was lying and kicked her until there was no movement. Casey then sprinted over and tried to untie Michael.

Alexis's goons were holding Markus and Xander back from the fight.

Alexis got up slowly and walked up to Michael. "Casey if you don't show yourself, I'll be forced to hurt, I'm guessing your lover."

Casey was still trying to untie Michael's hands when she said this, so Casey moved behind her and replied, "You lay another hand on him and you'll be sorry."

Alexis gave an evil laugh and started to swing to hit Michael.

Casey appeared beside her just in time, for Alexis to see a fist connect with her face.

Alexis flew backwards into a booth and when she regained her senses, she screamed, "It's time to end this," and when she got up, she started transforming into a brown and black wolf.

Xander had gotten away from the goons and stepped in front of Casey and yelled, "Alexis you know pack challenges are done in human form."

Alexis charged at him and he ended up flying into a wall. She turned to Casey and stalked towards her.

Casey backed up away from Michael so he wouldn't get hurt but Alexis took that as a sign of weakness and jumped at her.

Alexis connected with her shoulder and Casey went rolling across the floor.

While Casey was getting up, Xander woke up from hitting the wall and yelled, "Casey she cheated, now you can cheat."

Alexis charged Xander but before she could get to him, everyone heard a loud pop and she stumbled. She turned around and when she looked at Casey, blood was dripping out of her mouth. There were two more pops and Alexis fell to the floor with blood pooling around underneath her and a hole where her heart should've been.

Everyone turned and stared at Casey who was holding her gun.

Casey looked at Alexis who had converted back to human form. She looked down at the gun in her shaking hand, stunned at what she had done. She jumped when Xander put his hand on her shoulder. She looked up at him with tears in her eyes and whispered, "You said I could cheat."

Xander smiled and replied, "Yes, I did. Let's get you cleaned up."

Casey shook her head yes and looked around to see Angel getting medical attention and Michael being untied.

Xander sat Casey down at the bar and reached over for the first aid kit, while the other wolves moved Alexis's body and cleaned up the mess. He was silent while he patched up the claw marks on her shoulder and when he was done said, "Since you didn't know what a pack challenge was, I'm guessing you don't know what your win gets you."

Casey responded with a quick nod no.

"Technically your leader of the pack now."

Casey started laughing and said, "But I'm not a werewolf, I'm a witch."

Xander smiled and replied, "We aren't referred to as werewolves. They're so many types of animals you can shift into, we're simply known as shifters. Besides, you're not all witch, not with those yellow eyes."

They shared a look of concern and he continued, "And after this wound, you might be one of us."

Casey started to tear up again and said, "I can hope for the best. I can hope that I won't change. As for the pack, what if I let you run it for me in my absence? After all, you were Alexis's first lieutenant, why can't you be mine?"

"Sounds like a good plan to me, only if you're sure."

"It's a deal."

"If you need anything you let me know."

"You know me, I won't be afraid to ask. What about the other vampires?"

"Come by in a couple days, I'll have them ready."

Casey looked at him with an inquisitive look and he continued, "You don't even want to know what she did to them."

"Ok I won't ask," and he walked them out to the car and Casey drove them back to Buxton.

Once they got back to the trailer Markus took Angel to their room and took care of her.

Michael took Casey to their room. They put sheets on their bed without a word and fell asleep in each other's arms, not even concerned the sun was coming up to a new day.

Chapter Nineteen

Casey woke up to find she was the only one in the room. She got up and walked into the bathroom, started the water to take a shower and when she looked in the mirror; her sleepy gaze focused on the bandage that clung to her left shoulder. She undid the bandage and to her surprise the claw marks were almost healed.

There was a knock on the door and it was Michael. "After your shower come into the kitchen, I've made breakfast."

She heard him walk away before she could answer, so she jumped in the shower. She would've been quicker but she had so much dried blood from Angel, Michael and her own wound, it took some scrubbing to get it off.

Once clean, she went back to her room, put on some swimming trunk shorts and a tank top.

She walked into the kitchen where everyone was at and sat at the table to eat. In between bites she asked, "Has anyone called Jeremy?"

Angel spoke up, "Markus called him yesterday and told him what happened. I've never heard a happier vampire."

Casey stopped chewing and asked, "Wait, yesterday?"

Michael replied, "You've been asleep for twenty-four hours."

Casey choked on the eggs in her mouth and exclaimed, "I missed a whole day!"

Angel chuckled and replied, "Your body needed to heal."

Casey looked at Angel and said, "Speaking of healing, you heal nicely."

Angel smiled and said, "You do too for a human."

They both laughed.

Casey looked Angel up and down, there was not a mark on her. However, there were still marks left over on Michael and herself, which showed they were both still, partly human.

After breakfast, they went outside to sit on the deck and everyone was surprised when they saw about twenty vases of flowers, covering it.

All the cards had the same thing written on it; thank you, in big letters. None of them were signed, except the one from Xander.

This made Casey smile and feel better about what she had done. Even though she shouldn't have felt guilty, she did because it was the first life she had taken.

After some persuading, everyone decided Angel was right and they went to the beach. They spent all day, relaxing and swimming. Just before dark they came back to the trailer to watch a movie but fell asleep before it started.

They woke up the next day still in the same position on the couch.

It was about one in the afternoon when Casey looked at everyone and said, "Hate to do this but we need to clean house again. My parents will freak if I leave this place a mess."

Angel laughed and said, "You just went up against the most vicious bitch ever and you're scared of your parents."

Markus answered, "You don't know her folks."

Everyone snickered and they went about doing chores.

Chapter Twenty

It was a little bit before five o'clock when Angel and Casey gave up trying to get the blood off the sheets. They left and went to Conner's Market, to buy new ones.

Once in the store, Casey looked at Angel and said, "We have company, his scent is very strong."

They quickly bought the sheets and left without talking, so he wouldn't hear them. Once in the car, they sat and waited for him to come out and to their surprise, Ivey was following someone else, not them.

Angel and Casey drove back to the campground. When they walked into the trailer Angel said, "Would've been here sooner but Ivey was at Conner's and we had to dodge him."

Michael was angry and blurted out, "We can't get any peace from him can we. You remember what I told you, he does one more thing."

Casey, disgusted with the way he was acting, yet again, yelled, "He didn't even know we were there. I'm tired of this shit, Michael. There's so much more to worry about than your petty vendetta against Ivey."

She walked out the door, slammed it and took off running.

Michael tried to follow her but Markus stopped him and said, "Give her some time to cool down."

Michael stomped off to put the new sheets on the bed.

Chapter Twenty-One

Casey ran with no destination in mind. She just needed to burn off the anger she had towards Michael. She did not understand why he hated Ivey so much. He hadn't really done anything to them.

When Casey came back to reality, she realized she was on the new road that went to the lighthouse.

It was moved in 1999 because of the threat of shoreline erosion.

She turned around and continued at a jog to where it used to stand, took her shoes and socks off and walked towards the ocean. She walked the edge of the water trying to calm down. She had gone about a mile when she decided to sit down and take a break. She started thinking about everything that had happened and her shoulder started tingling. She then started thinking about turning furry and started to cry. She put her arms on her knees and her head on her arms.

Casey heard someone walking up and quickly wiped her tears away. She turned her head and saw Xander.

He sat down beside her, put his arm around her and leaned her into him.

With her head, still on his shoulder, she asked, "How have you always been able to make me feel better with just a hug?"

When she sat up, he smiled at her and replied, "I don't know. Maybe because we are what we are or we just feel safe with each other."

Casey sighed and said, "And you always know what I need ... Xander, what am I going to do? I don't want to turn furry ... oh shit, I'm sorry. No offense."

"None taken, it's not for some people. How did all of this start?"

Casey and Xander started walking back down the beach, as she explained. She told him about when Markus died, to when they came down to North Carolina. She included her powers, even them mingling with Michael's and the SIU.

Xander was stunned into silence. He hugged Casey and replied, "No wonder you're freaking out. This was way too much, way too soon. If there's anything I can do, please let me know. I hadn't heard anything from you and I was worried, that's why I came to find you."

"I'm sorry, how did you find me?"

"It might freak you out more."

"Xander, how?"

"Your scent. You're the leader of the pack now, we can find you by sniffing you out."

"Ok, yeah that's weird."

He laughed and said, "Hey, don't be too hard on Michael. He loves you and is just trying to protect you."

They hugged bye and Xander walked back to his car.

Casey sat down because she didn't want to go back and face Michael yet. She wasn't thinking about anything this time, just watching the surf come in and out. She was so focused on the ocean she didn't hear him coming up behind her, until she heard, "Is this seat taken?"

Casey looked up and saw Ivey sitting down beside her.

"What do you want?"

"Wanted to see how you were. I was walking down the beach trying to clear my head, when I saw you crying. You were talking to some guy and I didn't want to interrupt, so I waited until he left."

"Look I know Autumn and I saved you at the bar from Michael, but that was basically saving him from doing something stupid. You can't keep showing up like this. I'm not going to be around all the time to stop Michael from hurting you."

"I never did get a chance to thank you for that. I hope it didn't cause trouble between you and Michael."

"It did, but I can handle it. Autumn said something about you protecting me. Protecting me from what?"

"I wish she hadn't said anything."

Casey with a smile said, "Why? She was the one that talked me into not disliking you so much."

Ivey smiled back and replied, "She has always been such a sweet girl. She was my wife's little sister, ya know."

"She told me ... she also told me of the resemblance. If you don't mind me asking, what happened to your wife?"

Ivey paused and tears started building in his eyes when he replied, "Her name was Ariel and she was the love of my life. She was trying to stop someone from getting hurt. She wouldn't tell me who she was trying to protect, who she was trying to stop, or where she was going that night because she didn't want me to get hurt. I have a feeling who it was but I don't have any proof." He paused because he was getting choked up. A few minutes later he continued, "She called me while she was dying and used her last breath to tell me she loved me."

Casey saw a tear run down his cheek.

He turned to her and said, "I'm not trying to hurt you. Autumn was right, I'm trying to protect you from this person and please don't ask who it is. I want to get more proof so he can't deny it and right now, he doesn't know I'm on to him."

She turned to him, put her hand on his arm and said, "I believe you Jake and I won't ask."

His face lit up with a smile and he replied, "That's the first time you've called me by first name, since we met."

She smirked and said, "I'm sorry I've given you such a hard time, I'll be nicer."

"No, you can't. You can't give anyone, any reason to believe you know what I know. Your life may depend on it."

"Ok, so in public we'll keep up appearances."

"Sounds good to me."

Jake got up, helped Casey up and as they were walking to the parking lot she asked, "Why didn't you just tell us what was going on? Why did you act like you were trying to get information about Sidney?"

"I can sum it up in one word ... Michael."

"I understand, I had a feeling it was something like that."

Jake smiled and said, "I can drive you to the main road if you want."

Casey smiled back and replied, "No thank you, I need more time to think."

As he walked towards his car, Casey said, "Hey Jake."

He stopped and walked back to her as she said, "I need to tell you something about Sidney."

"What about her?"

"You know that I'm a witch ... well, one of my powers is to see the future. I had a vision on the last night I saw Sidney. I saw her in a corner of a dark room. She was bloody, dirty and someone was walking towards her. I couldn't make out who the person was and then the vision ended. I lied to you when I said I didn't know what happened to her and I'm sorry."

"You saw her in a corner, bloody and dirty. That's it ... it doesn't sound like you saw what happened to her."

"I guess not."

"Then you didn't lie to me." He closed the distance between them, put his arms around her and gave her a hug. When he pulled back he put one hand on each side of her face and kissed her forehead. He made eye contact with her and said, "Thank you for the talk and opening up to me."

She smiled and replied, "Thank you for opening up to me, too."

As he was getting into his car, he said, "Don't be too hard on Michael. He thinks I'm the bad guy and is just trying to protect you," and he finished sitting down and drove away.

Casey sat down and wiped the sand from her feet. She put her shoes and socks on and jogged back to the trailer.

Chapter Twenty-Two

Michael ran to Casey and grabbed her into a hug when she walked in.

"I'm sorry. I shouldn't have gone off like that. After everything we've been through the last couple days. It scared me when you shut the link completely like that, I couldn't sense you anywhere. I'm so sorry."

Casey hugged him back and replied, "I know you're just trying to protect me because you love me. I'm sorry I closed the link, I needed some space."

Michael pulled back, looked at her and replied, "What have you been doing the last couple hours, to be this calm? I'm not complaining but you were really mad at me when you left."

Casey kept the conversation she had between her and Jake a secret, for obvious reasons, and said, "I went walking on the beach to clear my head. I ran into Xander and we had a nice long talk."

As Michael and Casey walked back to their room, he said, "Remind me to thank him for, whatever, he said."

Casey smiled, if he only knew that the talk with Jake made her calm down more, he would hit the roof.

There wasn't much left for Casey to pack. She was almost done when Angel came into the room and said, "We need to talk."

"About what?"

"The fact you might turn furry on the next full moon."

Michael cleared his throat when he saw her facial expression and quickly said, "But you might not."

Casey said, "I have a fifty-fifty shot right, plus it isn't bad being furry, is it Angel?"

Angel replied, "Nope, the only bad part is going into heat."

Casey and Michael's jaw dropped.

Casey exclaimed, "Are you serious!"

Angel laughed and looked at Michael. "Hope you have good stamina."

She was laughing when she walked out the bedroom with Casey and Michael staring at each other in shock.

"Sounds like I'm in for a fun time."

Casey lightly punched his arm.

He caught her hand and pulled her into a long sensual kiss. While keeping her in the hug he said, "I'm with you no matter what."

Casey smiled, hugged him again and they took their bags out to the car.

CHAPTER TWENTY-THREE

It was seven o'clock by the time they got to the bar.

On the way, to ease Casey's mind, she called Jeremy and they discussed doing some testing to see what she was up against.

They walked in and saw Xander sitting in the booth across from the door in the corner.

Casey walked over, sat down by him and everyone else sat at the bar.

Xander was telling her he found out that Alexis had undercover agents in the SIU, when a waitress walked over with drinks.

She was a petite framed girl, with dark curly hair, just above her shoulders.

Casey stopped the conversation because she received a conflicting premonition from the drink, when she touched it. After the waitress left Casey asked, "Who's that?"

"That's Tia, one of our wolves and the waitress that pointed you out to us that night. She felt the power from your table, why?"

"I get a weird vibe from her ..." At that moment, she glanced across the room and saw Jake. Casey put her head in her hands and said, "That's it."

"What's it?"

"The vibe about Tia, it's the same vibe I had with Sidney. She has something to do with the Supernatural Investigations Unit."

"No ... she can't be. I didn't see her name on the list."

"If she's not SIU, she's hiding something from us about them, trust me."

"You're the boss; I'll keep an eye on her. I have someone I'm going to send up there to you, that's on the list, when he gets back. Alexis didn't like him and always had him away doing things, his name is Fitz. No objections, I want someone from your pack with you."

"Ok, no problem ... I have a question."

"Shoot."

They looked at each other and Casey said, "Ha ... ha ... why didn't the other wolves attack when I killed Alexis?"

"They were afraid of her ... the only way to explain it is, ding dong the witch is dead."

They both laughed and Xander excused himself to go get the vampires.

Michael walked over, sat down beside Casey and said, "You see who's sitting across the bar right."

"Yeah, our favorite agent."

"Yes, but look who's with him."

Casey looked over and couldn't keep the shock off her face. Casey looked back at Michael and asked, "What's Samson doing here?"

Samson is one of the wolves that came over with Angel and Markus. He's six-five and still had the massive body builder frame from the last time Casey saw him, however, he had exchanged his blonde ponytail for a buzz cut. He was sent undercover, by Jeremy, to see what information the SIU had on the supernatural beings' in Virginia.

"I don't know, see if you can get a read off him."

Casey looked over and got Samson's attention, suddenly Samson was in her head, *'I was told you could read thoughts, so I know you can hear me. Sidney didn't get a chance to rat me out and they moved me to the main branch. Please relay that to Jeremy. Ivey doesn't know why you're down here, he's here on other business. Just ignore him, however, let your wolf friend know to keep his nose clean until we leave tomorrow.'*

Casey gave him a nod and then looked back at Michael.

Xander came out of the office with two very young-looking vampires.

They both were male and identical twins. They were almost Casey's height, with a petite frame. They both had blonde, curly hair but only one had facial hair and it was a goatee.

When Xander introduced them to Casey, they both grabbed a hand and simultaneously kissed the back of them and said, "Thank you."

The one with the goatee was named Hunter and the other was Tyler.

Casey blushed and said, "You're welcome."

Xander said bye to everyone and Casey told him what Samson had said, as they were walking out the door.

They got in the Tahoe and headed back to Prince George, Virginia.

Chapter Twenty-Four

Casey woke up from a nightmare she was having of her killing Alexis, to an empty room. She collected herself, got up and as she was walking out of the room, she saw a note on the dresser.

It read, 'I couldn't bring myself to wake you up, you looked so peaceful. We're at the bar helping Bernie clean up from last night. I'll explain when you get here. Jeremy says to remind you that Leigh is coming today to draw your blood for testing. Love Michael.'

Casey put the note back on the dresser, took a quick shower, got dressed and was leaving fifteen minutes later. She drove to the bar singing along to the radio, trying to be optimistic about the testing.

When she pulled up to park, she saw Jake sitting in his car watching the building. She smiled and waved as she walked by.

Casey stopped as soon as the door closed and stood in disbelief of the damage done to the bar.

The mirror on the dance floor wall was shattered in one section. Parts of tables and chairs were all over the bar and there was trash all over the floor.

Michael saw Casey when he came out of the office and walked towards her. He was almost to her when she noticed him and said, "What the hell happened?"

"Agent Ivey and friends."

"He wasn't supposed to be home until today. How could he have done this?"

"Bernie said Xander called about an hour after we left. He overheard a phone call Ivey had, planning it. They came in a little after we left last night from dropping Hunter and Tyler off. Everyone was downstairs settling them in, when the agents came in and stayed there until they left. When they came upstairs this is what they saw."

"So, technically it wasn't J ... Ivey."

Michael gave her a strange look and said, "No, it was other agents but he had something to do with it, we'll talk about it later, Jeremy sensed you were awake and called Leigh. She should be here soon for your testing."

As they walked towards the office, Casey decided to keep to herself that Jake was sitting outside.

Casey and Michael walked into the office and sat on the couch.

Jeremy and Leigh came in through the basement door.

Casey looked up and exclaimed, "You're their DNA specialist!"

When Leigh shook her head yes, her brown curls bobbed up and down and her hazel eyes glistened, in the office light. She was about five-seven and it had been awhile since Casey had seen her, so Leigh's weight loss was a pleasant surprise. Other than their difference in height, they looked more alike now with the same build, after all they were family.

Jeremy and Michael had a perplexed look on their faces.

Casey continued, "I didn't think you would travel to the dark side."

Leigh laughed. "They pay too good to turn them down little sister."

Casey got up and they walked towards each other and gave a quick hug.

Leigh replied, "I had a feeling you were the one I made the serum for."

Casey nodded her head yes.

Jeremy exclaimed, "Wait a minute, you two are sisters?"

Casey and Leigh shook their heads yes and chuckled.

Jeremy continued, "I wonder how I didn't know that. We'll give you two some privacy."

Jeremy and Michael left the girls in the office by themselves.

Leigh took out a band, syringe, alcohol swab and empty vials. She put on her gloves, tied the band around Casey's arm and patted it to bring the veins out. She wiped a spot with the alcohol swab and picked up the needle.

Leigh said, "Ready?"

Casey shook her head.

A few minutes later, she had five vials of Casey's blood for testing.

As Leigh was putting up her stuff Casey asked, "Does Dad know, what's going on?"

"Yes, he does ... and what happened in Cape Hatteras."

"Wow, he can keep a secret, I thought I was going to have to tell him. Wait, how does he know?"

"Apparently, our big sister told him several months ago, she didn't want him or Mom to get hurt. She overheard a conversation from some agents, with our names included, and told him about us being involved."

"How did Ann know about North Carolina?"

"She didn't, that's where I come in. After he got off the phone with you, he called me to see what I did for them and to see if you had anything to do with it. Dad has always been able to catch us in a lie, plus he caught me off guard, with what he did know. So, I filled him in on what I knew and told him I didn't think it was you. Wasn't a complete lie but I didn't want them to worry about you. I realized at that moment, you may have been the one I made the serum for. You need to call and tell him you're fine."

Jeremy walked into the office as Casey was nodding.

Leigh looked at him and asked, "This is just routine testing, right?"

"Afraid not, I need a blood profile. We're looking for shifter qualities."

Leigh gasped, "Oh Casey, I didn't know who was attacked. I'll take extra precautions with these tests and have the results later today."

Casey tried to smile and got up to go help clean the bar.

Michael saw Casey's face when she walked out of the office. He made eye contact, saw she was crying and started walking towards her.

She popped into his head, '*I know you want to help, but consoling me right now will only make things worse.*'

'*I love you Casey.*'

'*I know.*'

Michael walked over to the DJ booth and put some music on. He apparently gave a signal to everyone else because nobody said anything to Casey, while they jammed for the next several hours, cleaning the bar.

Chapter Twenty-Five

When Jeremy came out of the office he was relieved at how fast the bar was back in shape. He sat down by Casey and said, "Leigh has the results of the tests, even ran them twice. She'll be here in ten minutes."

Casey sighed and replied, "I need a drink."

Michael had felt this coming and he walked over to Casey, with her favorite shot, already chilled.

Casey gulped it down and said, "Thanks."

They got up and finished putting the new table and chairs around the bar in their respective places.

When Casey sat back down, Jeremy walked up and said, "After you get the news from Leigh, I want you and Michael to take a couple days off. So, you can't make any excuses, it'll be a paid leave for both of you."

Casey snickered and nodded in agreement.

She put her head in her hands and started to massage her temples, thinking it might not be so bad turning furry. She realized that she'd be ok with whatever Leigh says.

When the bar door opened, Casey opened her eyes expecting to see Leigh but instead saw Jake. Casey had to play things normal and let out a small growl that Angel and Markus looked at each other about, and said, "Go away, you're not welcome here."

Jake waved Casey's remark off and replied, "The bar is open, correct?"

Jeremy nodded and directed a thought towards Casey, 'We *don't need any more trouble from him.*' Afterwards, Jeremy directed his attention back to Jake and said, "Sorry, what can I do for you Agent Ivey?"

"I just came to eat, don't mind me."

Jeremy motioned towards a booth for Jake to sit down and then motioned for the waitress to go and serve him.

Jake sat down, gave the waitress his order and then started to stare at Casey. He took off his necklace, hoping she'd take the hint and open the link between them. He thought, '*I didn't have anything to do with what happened last night. In fact, I tried to stop Paul and Alan from doing it.*'

Casey nodded.

He put his necklace back on and Casey felt the link close.

Angel and Markus were talking about the noise they heard come from Casey when she plopped down in the booth next to Angel, mumbling about Agent Ivey. When they stopped talking, Casey caught on and said, "You guys were obviously talking about me, what have I done now?"

Angel hesitantly asked, "How long have you been able to growl like that?"

"I growl all the time Angel, you know that."

"No, you don't growl like you use too."

Casey leaned her face on one hand and looked at Angel as she continued, "When we first met, you sounded like a human trying to sound like a dog, it was kind of funny. Now, there's no easy way to say it ... you sound like a ... well, like a wolf."

Casey's jaw dropped but before she could say anything, Jeremy passed by the table. He motioned for her and Michael, who was standing behind her, to follow him into the office.

CHAPTER TWENTY-SIX

Once in the office, they saw why he had them follow him, Leigh was back with the test results.

Casey asked, "What's the damage?"

Leigh sighed and said, "I'm not going to sugar coat this."

Casey replied, "Ok, go for it."

"I found two shifter qualities in your blood. The first one is wolf, which was given to you by the scratches from Alexis. The second one, I believe, because you had two different serums so close together; mingled with each other and that's what caused a feline shifter quality. It has been hidden until now and you haven't shifted because of your vampire abilities. You have four, non-human chromosomes wrapped around your original DNA; witch, vampire, wolf and feline. You don't have to worry about changing on the full moon because with your powers as a witch, you'll be able to shift whenever you want. You'll be more powerful than a regular shifter. Don't know when you'll change for the first time but I've heard of some sort of trigger, to provoke it. You just need to find your trigger and control it."

Casey sat there dumbfounded.

Jeremy and Michael didn't know what to say either.

After a few minutes of silence Casey said, "So, short and to the point; the serums and my powers as a witch, helped me but also doomed me. Not only am I a witch with vampire abilities; I'm a shifter that can form into a wolf or some type of cat, whenever I want."

Leigh answered, "Correct."

"Do you know how insane that sounds?"

"You're a strong person little sister. If anyone can handle it, you can."

Casey kind of laughed and just sat there staring, to let the information sink in. She heard the door shut, which shook her back to reality.

A single tear ran down her cheek when Michael put his hand on hers.

Casey got up, wiped the tear away and said, "No, I'm not going to cry. There's positive aspects about this situation ... right... who knows I might not change."

Michael got up, walked over behind Casey, put his arms around her waist and softly said, "I hate to be the bearer of bad news but you heard Leigh. She didn't say 'if' you would turn but 'when' you would turn. We just need to find your triggers."

"I know, I just don't know how to process the fact I'm going to turn furry. It wasn't real until now."

"I'll be at your side to help you through it."

"Thank you."

CHAPTER TWENTY-SEVEN

They walked out of the office to find Markus and Agent Ivey arguing.

Casey sat down with Angel, while Michael walked over to help Jeremy calm things down. Casey saw the inquisitive look on Angel's face and explained to her, what Leigh had told them.

Once it sank in, Angel replied, "Casey, I'm so sorry. I know you didn't want this." Angel patted Casey's hand and said, "There's something you need to know, I wasn't joking about wolves going into heat."

"Ha ... ha."

"I'm being serious now. When you go into heat, you need to have sex regularly, if you don't the consequences will be dire. If you fight the urge, it will get so bad you'll attack any man that shows interest in you, possibly even killing the man. Fighting the urge could also make you turn into your animal form. You should be with Michael as much as you can during that time, so the urge won't get out of control. You can go into heat at any time but the time you don't want to ignore, is the three nights of the full moon." She paused. "Casey, I haven't said anything because we didn't know for sure but the first night of the full moon, is tonight."

Casey looked at Angel and smiled. She shook her head and said, "It's always something."

Angel and Casey were laughing when Michael dragged Markus back over to the booth.

Casey looked up at Michael and he asked, "You ready to go home?"

"Yep, and we've got some things to talk about."

They said bye to everyone and walked out to the car. Before they left the parking lot, Casey informed him, what Angel had said.

The car ride home was very quiet, since Casey had to tune Michael's thoughts out.

It was his turn now to process this information.

CHAPTER TWENTY-EIGHT

When Casey and Michael got home, he went into the bedroom and she went into the kitchen, to call her dad.

No one answered, so she left a message, 'Hey Pop. The beach was a blast. Home safe, love you guys. Bye.' When she hung up, she went to the refrigerator and grabbed herself a Mic Ultra. She went to the living room and sat down to watch some TV.

Ten minutes later Michael called her back into the bedroom.

She walked into the room and he motioned her into the bathroom.

When she walked in, she saw candles on the counter and next to the tub, which was drawn into a bubble bath.

He said, "You need to relax after the news you received today and everything else you've had to deal with, the last couple days. I'll leave you alone for a bit."

Casey grabbed his arm as he walked out of the bathroom.

He turned around and she gave him a big hug, which brought out, "Casey, I can't breathe."

"Sorry, guess I don't know my own strength."

They smiled at each other and he left the bathroom.

Casey turned around, got undressed and climbed into the bubble bath. The water was warm and felt so good that she was relaxed in minutes.

Her thoughts consisted of happy ones, which included Michael. She came back to reality when she felt her stomach flutter. She heard Michael talking to someone but couldn't make out the conversation. She tried to read him but he had closed his thoughts to her.

Casey started pondering the thought of becoming furry and came to grips with it, after a bit. As she was thinking what it would be like to transform her stomach fluttered again. She noticed when she looked out the bathroom window, it was getting dark. She started to get a feeling in her stomach, of severe fluttering and it dawned on her what it was.

The moon was rising and Angel said going into heat would happen on the full moon, which was tonight.

She jumped out of the bath tub and looked at herself in the mirror, to make sure she wasn't becoming a wolf or cat, when Michael walked up to the door.

He asked, "Are you ok? Can I get you anything?"

Casey didn't answer, so Michael opened the door. He stopped because she was looking at him like he was a piece of food. He exclaimed, "Casey your eyes! Are you turning?"

Casey looked back in the mirror and saw for the first-time what Angel, Alexis and Michael had seen. Her eyes were bright yellow and in cat shape.

She gasped, "Michael in slow movements, shut the door and call Angel. Tell her what's going on and ask what stomach flutters mean."

Michael did as she asked and a few minutes later he knocked on the door. He replied, "She wants to know if you've had any more signs of changing, other than your eyes."

Casey looked at her body and face. "No."

He repeated the answer back in the phone and she heard him hang up. He walked back to the door and said, "Angel said not to worry, it's signs of going into heat for any shifter, it means your animal likes what it sees and ..."

"And what?"

"And for us to have fun."

Casey started laughing and then to her surprise let out a purr.

Michael gasped at the sound through the door and exclaimed, "What was that?"

Casey laughed again and replied, "I think kitty wants to come out and play."

The stomach flutters hit again when Casey opened the door and saw Michael.

His jaw dropped when he saw Casey standing in the doorway, naked with bubbles and water dripping off her body.

Michael was standing in front of the bed when Casey came out of the bathroom. He tried to step back but when he did, he fell onto the bed.

Casey took this time to pounce on Michael and ended up straddling his hips.

She started kissing his earlobe and then moved down to his neck. When she felt his body quiver, she switched to the other ear lobe and then down that side of his neck. She rose, still straddling his hips and grabbed the bottom of his shirt. She pulled it up towards his head and as it covered his face, and his arms were up, she stopped and pinned him. She started kissing around his left nipple and nibbled, until he gasped in pleasure. She kissed across to his right nipple and when she started to nibble, he caught her off guard by bucking and flipping her over.

He pinned her down with his legs, as he took his shirt off.

Before he could lay back down Casey was fumbling with his belt buckle and he straddled her with his hips, pinning her arms down to get her to stop.

When they made eye contact, he said, "My turn."

Casey smiled and started to purr when he returned the favor to both sides of her neck and both ears. He kissed her left breast and latched on to her nipple with a sucking motion.

Casey started wriggling and when Michael looked up her eyes had gone yellow again.

He hopped up and when he did, Casey jumped up on her knees, grabbed onto his jeans and ripped them off.

She grabbed him by his shoulders and threw him back on the bed. She straddled him again in squatting position and placed his rock-hard penis in her hand. She started to tease him with the head, rubbing it against the opening of her wetness. When she couldn't take anymore, she inserted him into her and raised up and down, with just the head inside. After a few strokes, she went all the way down to take him all in. She rode him slowly, taking him fully in, until he couldn't take anymore and flipped her over.

He put her legs over his shoulders and thrusted in and out of her soaking womanhood.

When Casey came, she screamed and grabbed the sheets because it had been building up for so long.

Michael gasped, he too was feeling the sweet release but also felt the warm gush from Casey. He placed her legs back on the bed and laid on top of her still inside. He caressed her hair and they shared a sensual kiss exploring each other mouths with their tongues.

When Michael shifted his hips, Casey said, "Uh-Oh!"

He saw her facial expression and exclaimed, "Again!"

"If you don't stop moving."

Michael pulled out of Casey quickly, trying not to turn her on because he needed time to recoup.

Casey walked into the bathroom, drained the tub and refilled it with warm water. As she was climbing in, Michael walked into the bathroom and her stomach fluttered. She stopped and turned to face him.

The look he saw on her face, he knew it was time again. He had anticipated this and was harder than he was, the first time. He grabbed her like he was going to hug her, spun her around and bent her over.

Casey was extremely wet from the first time and he slid right in. She was still tight which made them both moan, on every stroke.

No matter how much Casey wanted to take over, Michael wouldn't let her and she tried. She was so weak from the amount of orgasms, she had no strength to fight back.

They ended up coming at the same time, and this time the gush of fluid came out like a waterfall and went down both of their legs.

Michael didn't stay in after he released, so he wouldn't excite her again.

She stood up and when she turned around, he hugged her and said, "You, going into heat is either going to be the best thing that happened to me, or it's going to kill me."

Casey laughed.

They both climbed into the bath tub and took turns cleaning each other off; which surprisingly didn't stimulate Casey again.

They got out of the bath tub and when Casey walked into the bedroom, she saw that Michael had picked out a dressy outfit and had laid it on the bed.

When Michael walked into the bedroom Casey pointed to the dress and asked, "What's this for?"

"I have a surprise for you. I'm taking you out to dinner."

Casey smiled and hugged Michael, this time he could still breathe.

They both got dressed and thirty minutes later were walking out the door.

CHAPTER TWENTY-NINE

The moon was shining bright when they walked outside but it didn't have any impacts on Casey, which made her happy.

Michael wasn't in a hurry, so he took the long way and drove through Hopewell, into Colonial Heights and turned onto the Boulevard. He turned into the parking lot of Wagstaff Steakhouse and parked the car.

They got out of the car and walked into the restaurant. The hostess seated them in the corner, over-looking Swift Creek.

For the next two hours, they sat eating, drinking and talking about each other's lives. They both told the good, the bad, and the ugly, holding nothing back. When they left, they were arm in arm and he even opened her car door.

He was being very romantic tonight and it was making Casey want him more than ever.

As they drove back home, they held each other's hand and Casey thought about what she wanted to do to him, when they got home. She kept the link between Michael and her closed, so he wouldn't see what was coming.

She remembered Markus and Angel weren't going to be home because of the full moon and they would have the house to themselves.

When they walked in, Casey turned around and jumped on Michael wrapping her legs around his waist.

They bounced off the door kissing and stumbled backwards to land on the coffee table, which shattered. That didn't stop them as they tore each other's clothes off and Michael tossed her on the couch.

Her ass was hanging off the edge, so Michael crawled over and opened her legs. He took turns inserting his finger and playing with his tongue.

Casey cried out a few minutes later, "I need you in me now!"

Michael stood up on his knees, slid his solid member into Casey and stopped.

Casey smacked his arm and yelled, "Stop teasing."

He smiled and slowly pulled out and pushed in a few more times.

Casey moaned and wrapped her legs around his waist and plunged him inside her.

They both moaned and she let him take over, pumping in and out of her saturated womanhood.

As he was doing this, he rubbed just above her opening with his thumb, which made her squirm with pleasure. When he felt her about to come again, he pulled out and said, "I want this to last a little longer."

Casey needed the sweet release, she popped up and threw him on the couch. She mounted him and he glided right back in. She grabbed the back of the couch and shifted back and forth, riding him, until he came with such force; Casey swore she felt it in her stomach. She stayed seated on him, so she could catch her breath.

Michael didn't give her that chance. He picked her up still inside her, still as hard as he could be and carried her back to the bedroom, to surprise her with another round. This time he said it was going to be slow and sensual. He laid her down on the bed and slowly stroked in and out.

Her muscles were so tight from the other times, it didn't take long for them both, to release again. When her muscle stopped convulsing, Michael quickly retreated and collapsed beside her on the bed.

They cuddled together too tired to do anything else.

Casey fell asleep propped up on his shoulder and he fell asleep to her purring.

Chapter Thirty

Casey and Michael woke up to someone yelling their names. They both got up, threw on their robes and ran out into the living room. As they rounded the corner they saw Angel and Markus.

Angel replied, "We saw the coffee table and wanted to make sure you both were ok."

Casey and Michael looked at each other and smiled.

Angel and Markus knew right away, what had happened to the table.

Markus helped Michael clean it up, while Angel and Casey went into the kitchen.

As they were cooking breakfast, Angel asked, "So, how many times last night?"

"Four."

"Four!"

"Why is that not normal?"

"The first night is always the roughest, but four ... well, at least tonight will be less, that's if you even need any."

"That's cool, I'm a little sore today."

They both laughed.

A few minutes later the eggs and toast were done.

They all ate in silence because of how hungry they were but also because they didn't know what to say.

Once they were done, Markus and Angel went to bed.

Michael and Casey, went to the bedroom and she changed the sheets, while he took his shower.

Casey took her shower afterwards and when she was done, they cuddled back in bed and went to sleep.

They woke up at sundown to find Markus and Angel already gone for the night.

Casey and Michael decided to get dressed to go to Nocturnal for the first time, as a couple.

When they got to the bar it was seven o'clock.

Michael parked the Tahoe behind the bar, which was a good thing because Casey started to have flutters in her stomach again.

Casey blurted out, "Michael!" Apparently, she didn't need to say anymore.

Michael got in the back seat and as Casey joined him, she said, "Thank goodness for tinted windows."

They both laughed and de-clothed from the waist down. They couldn't get a good position, until he placed her over the back seat.

He didn't need to prepare her, she was already wet. He entered her swiftly and she gasped with enjoyment. He shoved in and out, until they both came with such force they both cried out in satisfaction.

Luckily, Casey had a bag of dry cleaning in her car and that's what they used to clean themselves off.

They found the back door locked, so they started walking around the front of the bar, when Ivey grabbed Casey's arm and turned her around.

Ivey said, "Wish you were my girlfriend. Would love to have sex in a car."

Michael started coming towards them, when Casey yanked her arm from Ivey's grip, which wasn't too hard and smacked him in his face.

"You know I can take you in for that."

"Then take me in, I don't care."

"I think I'm going to let you owe me a favor, instead."

Before Casey could speak, Ivey walked away laughing. She dragged Michael the rest of the way and into the bar.

They said hi to everyone, ordered food and went to the last pool table that was open.

They had started their third game when Casey sensed an unfamiliar shifter in the bar and felt him staring at her. She looked around but couldn't find the culprit.

They finished their game by the time the waitress had brought their food. They took their plates and went to eat out on the patio.

Casey took that time to tell Michael what she had sensed.

Michael told her she worried too much and to forget about it, there new shifter's in the bar every night.

She did until she sensed the shifter come out on the patio. She looked towards the door and saw a guy with dark hair and green eyes, walking out.

He was about six-two and was an average build. There was nothing special about him, in fact, if he didn't smell like a shifter she wouldn't have noticed him.

When Michael got up to go to the bathroom the guy looked at him, then at Casey.

He walked over to Casey and said, "My name is Fitz. What's yours?"

"Casey."

"It took me a little bit to sense you out, I thought your friend was the shifter. It wasn't until he left ... he has your scent all over him."

"He's my boyfriend."

"You have a human boyfriend? Aren't you afraid you'll hurt him with you being a shifter?"

"Well, I'm different than most shifters."

"Oh ... are you Casey Rickman?"

"The one and only."

"I heard what happened in North Carolina, I was out of town on business." He paused, sniffed the air and continued, "I'm getting several scents from you ... what you are?"

"Who the hell are you and how do you know who I am?"

"I'm sorry, technically, you're my boss. I'm Xander's first lieutenant and that makes me your second lieutenant."

"Sorry, with everything going on, I forgot that Xander was sending someone up here. I'm just a very suspicious person, these days ..."

Casey didn't see Jake walk up and he interrupted, "She is very suspicious but she's not a person. She's not the type of girl you want to mess with."

Casey jumped up, faced him and said, "You know what, I'm tired of you. The stunt you pulled outside crossed the line Jake. I thought we had an understanding." She balled up her fist and punched him square in the nose.

Casey was approached from behind and heard, "Don't fight, I'm SIU and you're under arrest for assaulting an agent."

Casey was being walked to the door when Michael came back from the bathroom, in handcuffs.

She said, "Michael that's Fitz, he'll explain what happened."

Casey was ushered out by Ivey and the other agent stayed in the bar.

Chapter Thirty-One

Ivey put Casey in his car and as they drove to the station he said, "I had to bring you in, I needed to talk to you. Paul has been watching you and planned on doing something to you tonight. I couldn't find out what, so I had to improvise. That's the reason for the comment behind the bar. I knew it would piss you off enough to do something to me."

"Paul huh. Well, you better be glad Michael didn't do anything first."

"I knew you wouldn't let him because of our conversation at the beach. That's why I waited until Michael left, to approach you."

"Even though you went about this the wrong way, thank you for watching out for me."

"Your welcome."

"Next time though, can you fill me in on what's going on first."

"No problem."

"Jake, we need to tell someone what's going on before one of us gets hurt."

"I don't know who I can trust. So, for now, please keep this between us."

"For now, but if it becomes too dangerous we're telling someone. Deal?"

"Deal!"

They pulled up to the station, he turned around, smiled and said, "We need to make this look good. Just know I'm sorry for what I'm about to do." He got out of the car, grabbed her arm and yanked her out. He pushed her all the way to the interrogation room, sat her down and left.

A six-three muscular man entered the room. He had a buzz cut with blonde hair, piercing blue-green eyes and was wearing black dress pants and a blue collared shirt.

Casey sensed he was human and it dawned on her, this may be the guy that let her and Angel out of interrogation, back in January.

"Ms. Rickman. I'm Agent Temple, Ivey's boss. I saw him bring you in. Do you know why?"

"I had enough of his shit and I hit him."

"Oh ... ok. Look you might be able to help. I have an agent watching you and Ivey. You might have met him tonight; his name is Fitz. I know he's your second lieutenant but he doesn't report what happens in the clan. It was my idea to keep it a secret from you, so don't be mad at him. I haven't told him anything about you and as you may have guessed, he has something special about him. I needed that type of person because Ivey has lost it. He is obsessed with you and I wanted you to have protection. I know what you are and I know you don't think you need it, but better to have it then not. We also need more proof, so we can make him take medical leave. I don't want any trouble with you and your people at Nocturnal. I believe we can co-exist together and if you can help that would be great."

Casey realizing, Jake had not filled his boss in on what was going on asked, "What can I actually do?"

"Keep a record of when you see him what he says, that sort of stuff."

As Casey hesitantly nodded her head Jake walked back in and said, "I was looking for you boss. I brought her in because she hit me but we can question her about the other situation too."

Temple got up, shook his head no and replied, "She apologized for punching you and I'm not so sure, you didn't deserve it. Ms. Rickman you're free to go, sorry for the inconvenience."

"No problem."

As Casey walked away she heard Temple tell Ivey, they needed to talk.

When Casey walked out of the police station, Michael was waiting for her, in the Tahoe.

She climbed in and had to explain to him what happened with Temple because she had the link closed between them.

Michael didn't like just sitting back and taking notes but reluctantly agreed with Casey, to leave Ivey alone and let Agent Temple handle it.

When Casey and Michael got home, before they could go into the house, Agent Ivey's car pulled up across the street and turned off.

Michael rolled his eyes and said, "You've got to be kidding me!"

Casey smiled because she knew he was just protecting her.

They went inside and Casey called the number Charlie had given her for Samson and left a message about Agent Temple.

She hung up the phone and five minutes later it rang. When she picked it up, Samson's voice was on the other end and he said, "Can't talk, Temple is sincere. You can trust him," and the phone went to dial tone.

Casey hung up and told Michael what he said.

They climbed in the bed and fell asleep in each other's arms, too tired to do anything else.

Chapter Thirty-Two

The next morning, Casey woke up with her arms and legs intertwined with Michael. She watched him sleep because he looked so peaceful. She maneuvered to see the clock and it was two in the afternoon.

The phone rang ten minutes later, which woke him up.

When Casey answered it, Jeremy was on the other line. She said the occasional 'yes sir' and 'it's ok' and then hung up.

She rolled over and lightly rubbed Michael's cheek with the side of her finger.

Michael moaned, "I don't want to get up."

"I don't either, but Jeremy needs us to come in and set up for some sort of convention tonight and to work."

He sat up and asked, "Are you going to be able to with the full moon tonight?"

"The last two nights should've been sufficient. Jeremy knows what's going on, so if I start to get the flutter's, I'll call you."

Michael laughed, climbed out of bed and walked into the bathroom to take a shower.

Casey decided while he was in the shower to join him and feed the need, just in case.

After having some fun, they took a shower, got dressed and as they left the house, saw Agent Ivey.

Michael waved.

Casey rolled her eyes, sighed and said, "Don't antagonize him."

"Sorry couldn't help it."

They drove to the bar with Ivey following them.

Ivey stayed in his car, while Michael parked in the back and they made their way inside.

Jeremy and the other vampires were sitting at the bar talking. When he saw them, he said, "I called you two in because I need heavy hitters tonight. As I said there's a convention coming in, but this isn't just any people coming tonight. The bar is closed to humans and it's going to be shifters and our vampires. I've made a list of what needs to be done. I'll be in my office if you need me." He handed Casey the list, she read over it and delegated tasks.

"Julia and Elizabeth, you get everything straight in here. Bernie, go downstairs and bring up extra cases of beer and liquor. Michael and I will get the patio straight."

Everyone nodded, Elizabeth saluted and went to work without saying a word.

Casey and Michael went out to the patio and started taking down the covers, that kept the windows closed. They took inventory of the alcohol needed and Michael went inside to get it.

As Casey was straightening up behind the bar, Fitz came up outside the patio and leaned against the railing.

Casey smelled him before she saw him and when she turned around he said, "Hello Ms. Kitty."

Casey smirked and replied, "Hey Mr. Agent. I see you figured out one scent."

"I was going to tell you, I just didn't have a chance."

"I'm not mad, Xander filled me in on what you do. I'm actually relieved to have the protection and that we can co-exist with SIU."

"Now they know we aren't a threat, there's no need to worry about them. As for your other comment, I have figured out one scent but the other is masked by a lot of power."

Casey smiled, looked past him and said, "Here we go again."

Fitz turned around and saw Ivey walking up.

Ivey asked, "Is this guy bothering you Casey?"

Casey looked at him with a scowl and said, "Nope, but you are."

Jake acted pissed off and blurted out, "But he's SIU too."

Fitz stood up with a smile on his face looking at Casey and she simply said, "I know about his job, he's not here to cause trouble."

Fitz smirked and Ivey stormed off.

Casey replied, "It was probably not a good idea to piss him off more."

"Don't worry about Ivey, he's harmless." He leaned back down on the rail and asked, "How much do you know about my job?"

"Xander told me you were SIU and here for my protection. When I was taken in last night, Agent Temple, pretty much told me the same thing. I just acted like it was the first time I heard it. It's nice to have another feline around the bar, amongst the wolves."

Fitz cocked his head to the side, smiled at her and replied, "At least you don't have to worry about him in the bar tonight. You must be let in on the sensation of being a shifter, no humans allowed. In fact, you might want to watch your honey, since he's going to be the only human in the bar tonight."

"Michael can handle himself, unless you know something I don't."

"Well it's just … it gets a little wild on the last night of the full moon."

Michael came out with a box in his hands. "Hey Fitz, what brings you here so early? Party doesn't start for another hour."

"I was contracted by Jeremy to help with security."

"Then get your ass in here and help setup."

Fitz laughed and hopped the wooden fence.

Michael pointed towards the door and said, "They're more boxes inside."

Fitz walked towards the door while Casey started sweeping and Michael unpacked the box he had brought out.

After everything was unpacked, they went inside, ordered dinner and sat at one of the booths.

While they waited for their food Fitz asked, "What did Temple tell you about Ivey?"

"He told me that Ivey was obsessed with me and he had lost it, but you needed more proof to do anything about it. He said that's where I came in, to keep a record of what Ivey does and says when he's around me."

"Well, with the rate that Ivey's going, it won't be too long before we have the proof against him."

"Did you ever think ... maybe something else is going on?"

"If there is, Ivey needs to tell someone."

The conversation was dropped when their food was brought to them. As they started eating, Jeremy came out of the office and called for everyone's attention.

"This is how tonight is going to work. My security team is Michael, Julia, Bernie, Elizabeth, and Fitz. Fitz is on loan tonight from Casey's clan in North Carolina. There will be five spots around the bar you'll shift too during the night, and they are; the door, outside on the patio, by the stage, by the pool tables, and one walking around. You'll draw from a hat to see where you start. Casey you're behind the bar on the patio, we'll keep that open for a short time. Everyone else will pick whether they want to waitress or be behind the bar in here. I have one last thing to say and this is important. There will be shifting tonight and the only person I'm worried about is Michael. Since Casey is part shifter, I believe she can take care of herself. However, they'll think Michael is human and he might need some help fending off the shifters, when they first shift. Michael, I know you don't want help but remember, they won't smell that your part vampire. So please take it."

Michael shrugged his shoulders and continued eating.

Jeremy went back into the office.

Casey heard, '*Part vampire, that smells like a human, with a shifter. I'm not asking about that.*'

She looked at Fitz and sighed, nodding her head side to side.

He didn't know what her reaction was about and shrugged his shoulders.

Everyone finished eating and then checked over their designated section, one last time.

CHAPTER THIRTY-THREE

The bar opened at six o'clock and when Casey walked out to the patio to recheck her section, she saw a line of people waiting to get in. She took a deep breath and couldn't believe the different scents, swirling in the air.

The patio door popped open and out came Fitz. He said, "This is my first duty station."

"Cool, I have some questions about shifting I want to ask you before I get too busy."

"I'm an open book, what do you want to know?"

"Does it hurt?"

Fitz smiled and replied, "There's a little discomfort but it's not a bone popping change like in the movies. It's more like ... like a magic show, one minute you're human and the next, you're an animal. The change happens so fast, there's only a little pain. Wait, it's the third night of the full moon and you haven't changed, I don't understand."

"Long story short, I can change whenever I want because of my powers."

"Holy shit, you're a witch too. That explains why I couldn't figure out the other scent. Now I know to push those powers aside," he paused and took a deep breath. "I sense ... wolf."

"Xander didn't tell you about me?"

"No, he likes to test me, keep me on my toes. I knew Alexis attacked you, but when I couldn't smell wolf; I thought maybe you didn't get infected. So, let me get this straight, you're a witch, wolf shifter and have some type of feline shifter in you."

"Yep, I'm a triple threat."

They both laughed.

"Casey, only the most powerful shifters can change when they want too. You're going to be highly sought for in tonight's activities."

Casey stopped what she was doing and hesitantly asked, "What do you mean?"

"The last night of the full moon, all the shifters meet and it's pretty much a mating night. The only time shifters keep the baby full term, is when they conceive in animal form."

Casey gasped, "Sorry to inform you, I won't be shifting tonight. Michael is the only one I'm interested in "mating" with and that'll be kept in private."

"There's going to be a lot of disappointed feline's or wolves tonight and I have to say, I'm one of them."

Casey gave him a shame on you look and started getting her first customers. As Casey served drinks, she dealt with stares and whispers.

Fifteen minutes later, Michael came out the door, sat at the bar and Fitz gave him a nod as he walked past him to go inside.

Michael saw Casey had a moment and asked, "Has it been busy out here?"

"In spurts, I think they just want to see what I'm like. I'm a bit of a freak, even too shifters."

"What have you had to deal with?"

"Just whispers and stares," and she started getting customers again.

Chapter Thirty-Four

Bernie stuck his head out about eight and said, "Jeremy wants you to shut this bar down and come inside to the office. Michael, you're to be another floater."

Casey shut down the bar, counted the till and Michael escorted her through the many stares and seductive looks too the office.

Only Casey went into the office and to her surprise Xander was sitting on the couch.

He got up and gave her a hug, after she put the till down on the desk.

She looked at him and said, "You too for the mating game, huh?"

Xander laughed and replied, "No, just here to keep an eye on our wolves."

"Sorry, didn't mean to assume."

"It's ok."

"Xander, we can trust Fitz, right?"

"Yeah, he's your second lieutenant and he's SIU protecting you from this Ivey person. It was a decision I made to help you."

"I know, I just want to make sure we didn't have another spy."

"Nope, he's good and if anything, he's spying on the SIU for us."

Casey looked at Jeremy and asked, "Where do you want me?"

"I've got enough behind the bar but they could use you as a waitress until the shifting occurs."

Casey nodded and walked out to the bar to get her section.

Thirty minutes later, Casey sensed something was about to happen. As she turned around from the bar, several people fell to the floor and reappeared as all sorts of animals. Casey looked around searching for Michael.

He was at the patio door with Bernie, who was standing in front of him, protecting him from a solid black wolf.

Casey started to make her way over to help Bernie, when a Bengal Tiger blocked her path.

It was utterly beautiful and wouldn't let her pass. It swatted at Casey and she gave a low growl. It rubbed up against her leg, like a common cat and she had a premonition of who the tiger was; as a human.

She put her hand over her mouth, squatted down in front of the tiger and was face to face with it, when she said, "Fitz."

Fitz's eyes lit up and he gave her a quick lick on her cheek.

Casey scratched the sides of his face and said, "If you can understand what I'm saying, think the answer."

The tiger cocked his head to the side and thought, '*I can understand you.*'

"I need you to go and help Bernie protect Michael. I'm assuming you can get there quicker, then I can."

'Yes *ma'am.*'

He turned around and jumped and dodged through the sea of wolves, lions, tiger's, leopards, and even a black panther.

Casey started making her way over and this time she was rubbed up against by a brown wolf. She had a flash of the waitress Tia and nudged her to the side. Tia growled and Casey stopped to growl back, which made the wolf back off.

When she looked up, Bernie saw Casey's face, got Michael's attention and pointed towards her.

Michael gasped, "Holy shit! Those aren't her cat eyes."

They lost Casey in the horde of animals, so they paid attention to their fate.

The need to protect Michael came over Casey. She stumbled to her knees, went invisible and fell to the floor. An overwhelming amount of fear coursed through her body and she began to feel body parts and organs moving. When she got up something was different, she felt like she was crawling. She looked at what was supposed to be her hand and saw a paw, covered in red fur.

When she reappeared to everyone else, she was bounding towards Michael and Bernie. She leaped across the other shifters, landed in front of the guys, turned around and growled at the animals.

Bernie was about to hit the Red Wolf when Michael stopped him.

"It's protecting us, just like the tiger."

The Red Wolf snarled and growled at the other animals, with help from Fitz. This combined with the power radiating from the Red Wolf, made the animals back off and leave Michael alone.

Once the threat was over, the wolf walked over to Michael and rubbed against his leg.

He went to his knees and brought the wolf's face towards him and said, "Thank you, whoever, you are."

'*You're welcome, babe.*'

Michael gasped, "Casey!"

She licked him straight up the middle of his face.

Michael laughed and replied, "You make a beautiful wolf."

'*Thanks babe. Tell Bernie I'm taking you to the office.*'

Michael told Bernie what was happening and as they started moving towards the office, the most sensational thing occurred.

Every shifter they passed, bowed.

Chapter Thirty-Five

Casey sauntered into the office with Michael and Bernie. She laid down on the floor, while Jeremy sat amazed.

Jeremy asked, "Is that, who I think it is?"

Michael nodded his head, sat down on the couch next to Casey, who was in sitting position now and laid her head in his lap.

It took a minute, but Xander said, "Oh shit, is that Casey! I've only heard about Red Wolves, I've never seen one. Red Wolves are so rare they're considered royalty; most shifters have never seen one."

Bernie pointed at Michael and said, "That could be why they were still growling at you. They were testing Casey." Bernie paused. "Also, could be why they bowed when you walked by. They realized what color she was and felt her power."

Xander leaned over to rub Casey's head but she moved over and leaned up against his leg.

He put his hand under her chin, raised her face so they were looking each other in the eyes and replied, "You're magnificent, absolutely gorgeous."

Casey rubbed up against his legs.

Xander jumped and blurted out, "Casey stop! You don't know what you're getting ready to do."

Casey stopped rubbing, sat in front of him but looked at Michael. Michael asked, "She wants to know what you mean?"

Xander explained, "Pack leaders can force members of their pack to change, whether it's a full moon or daytime. The rubbing is how it starts, your power was starting to build. If you hadn't stopped, when it released it would go to your nearest pack member or members and forces the change. It can be very dangerous to everyone involved, if done wrong."

Casey looked at Michael, then back at Xander, put her head on his knee and looked up at him.

"She's very sorry and will be careful from now on. She wants to know why you haven't changed for tonight?"

"I've been a shifter for a long time. If I change the first two nights of the full moon, I can choose to change or not change for the last night. I knew I was going to be watching our wolves and I wanted to be human for it."

"She says thank you for watching over them and again she's sorry."

"No worries, it's my job and stop apologizing, you didn't know."

Jeremy piped up. "There's a lot she's going to need to learn. Luckily, she has you and Fitz to teach her. Michael take her home, go out the back way through the basement, to avoid a scene."

Chapter Thirty-Six

Casey hopped up in the back of the Tahoe, not only was she too big, there was no way to explain having a wolf in your front seat.

As they drove away Casey thought, '*So, what do I look like?*'

Michael laughed, thought for a minute and replied out loud, "When I saw you trying to make your way over, your eyes were a bright green. You disappeared and the next time I saw you, was when I realized it was you protecting me. You're as big as a bear but your fur is a little longer and so soft. You make a gorgeous wolf." He paused for a minute and asked, "What were you feeling when you turned?"

'*I had this overwhelming feeling to protect you. I believe that's what made me go invisible. I went to my knees and then a feeling of fear and not being able to control anything came over me. That's probably what made me turn into my wolf form. If those feelings trigger those two powers, I wonder what I'll feel when I turn into my cat form.*'

"What happens when you're in animal form?"

'*I'm myself, just can't talk.*'

"It was some night, huh."

'Yeah it was. I'm not tired though. I think I'm going to go try and find Markus and Angel.'

Michael nodded and replied, "Be careful," and when they pulled up to the house he got out of the car and opened the hatch back.

Casey jumped down, rubbed against Michael about knocking him down and ran off towards the tree line. When she reached the woods, she turned around and thought, *'I love you Michael.'*

She heard back, *'I love you too,'* and disappeared into the woods.

CHAPTER THIRTY-SEVEN

Casey had been running for a while, enjoying the freedom. She slowed down to a walk looking around the forest through her wolf eyes. She was amazed how everything was so vivid, how far she could see and the colors of everything. She was amazed with her sense of hearing too, she could hear other animals and cars from a mile away.

She found an opening to a road but decided not to cross to the other side. She laid down behind a large log, this way if someone came down the road she would be hidden.

She stayed there for a while admiring her furry body. She played around, extending and retracting her claws. She took her tongue and touched her fangs and other teeth. When she got up to leave, she heard a car coming so she crouched back down behind the log.

The car stopped and turned the lights off. A few minutes later, another car pulled up beside it and did the same thing. Both occupants got out of their vehicles and walked around to stand in front of the first car.

To Casey's surprise she recognized both men. Paul was standing right in front of her, with Alan. They were SIU agents she met in January, when they were undercover with Jake.

Paul stood at six feet with a stocky build and had his head shaved.

Alan was six-two with short blonde hair. He was stockier than Paul, but not by much.

In fact, both had put on muscle since the last time she had seen them.

Casey never liked either of the men and them being out here, could not be good in anyway. She listened to their conversation.

"Paul, I don't understand, why we're still going after him? I understand Casey and everyone at Nocturnal, they had something to do with Sidney's untimely departure. However, Jake didn't have anything to do with that. Even trashing the bar back fired on us."

"He's trying to protect her just like he tried to protect his wife. I think he took her into the station the other night because he knew we were up to something. I can't have him protecting her like that, she needs to pay for her part in my girlfriend's disappearance. Sidney told me she was scared for her life and if they found out who she was, no one would ever see her again. They've done something to her, I just don't have any proof."

"I know, but don't you think killing his wife was punishment enough for Jake?"

The confession startled Casey and when she tried to sneak away, she stepped on a dead branch and snapped it. She stopped in her tracks and slowly turned her head towards the men.

They had their guns drawn with flashlights, heading straight for her.

She took off running towards home and heard a gunshot. Her adrenaline was pumping so hard, she didn't feel getting hit.

After what seemed like forever, she finally saw the tree line that lead to her house. As she was reaching it, she started feeling woozy. When she slowed her speed down, she felt a sharp pain in her right shoulder. The sun was coming up as she stumbled out of the woods. She made it to the driveway, collapsed on the ground and felt her body parts and organs shifting back to human form. Luckily, it's not at all like the movies and she had retained her clothes.

She tried to get up and couldn't, she tried to crawl and couldn't do that either. However, what she did do, was pass out from the pain.

Chapter Thirty-Eight

Fitz was finishing up working security when he stumbled into the office and he looked at Xander.

Xander stood up quickly and as they were sprinting out the door he blurted out, "Casey's hurt."

Jeremy showed Fitz out the back door and he took off running.

Xander left the office at the same time, ran to his truck and sped off towards Casey's house.

Fitz bounded through the woods, dodging trees, low limbs and bushes. When he was clearing the tree line from the other side of the yard, he saw Casey stumble out of the woods, collapse in the driveway and change back.

As he was running through the field, he felt his return to human form start but had plenty of practice and didn't miss a step changing back.

She was already unconscious by the time he reached her.

It wasn't very hard to see where she was injured. She had blood pooled around her shoulder, stuck to her shirt and blood stains going down her right arm.

As he bent down to roll her over, Xander came peeling down the driveway. He threw the truck in park and jumped out, to help pick her up.

Michael had heard the commotion and was running outside, as they reached the front door.

"Oh, shit! What happened?"

Fitz carried her in and put her on the couch replying, "She's been shot."

Michael was mad and yelled, "How did that happen? Who did this to her?"

Xander calmly replied, "Getting angry isn't going to help Casey right now. We were still at the bar when Fitz felt her get hurt and got here as soon as we could. We found her in the driveway."

Michael started to panic and asked, "Is she going to be ok? Why hasn't she healed, yet?"

Fitz replied, "There's no exit wound, the bullet is still in her shoulder. Michael, I need alcohol, tweezers and towels."

Michael went to get what Fitz needed and Xander went to help.

As Fitz was ripping Casey's shirt to get to the bullet wound, she whispered, "Damn, I loved this shirt."

A smile came across his face and he said, "Hey beautiful, glad to see your awake. You're not going to like what I'm about to do. I need to take the bullet out."

Casey growled, and said, "Ok. Afterwards, I need you to do something for me."

"What?"

Just as Casey said, "I need you to contact Agent Temple and Agent Ivey, tell them to come here now. I was shot because I overheard a conversation," Michael and Xander walked back into the living room with the supplies for Fitz.

"I promise, someone will call them. Now, I need you to roll over on your stomach. Can you do that for me?"

Casey tried her hardest but couldn't manage.

All three guys helped roll her over, so she wouldn't hurt herself more.

Fitz put his hand on the small of her back, leaned closer and said, "Casey this is going to hurt like a sum bitch. Michael come over and hold her hand."

Michael walked over, sat on the floor, kissed her forehead and held her hand.

When Fitz poured the alcohol on her wound, she let out a blood curdling scream and about ripped Michael's hand off. She was crying and squirming so bad, that Xander had to hold her legs.

"I'm going to get the bullet out now Casey."

She braced herself but wasn't ready for the searing pain that came next. She screamed again and went silent. Before she went out she saw the door open and Markus and Angel came running in.

Xander explained to them what they knew while Fitz finished fishing the bullet out.

Angel went to call Agent Temple to get him and Ivey there, before Casey woke up.

Once the bullet was removed, her arm started to heal.

As Michael and Fitz were cleaning up her arm, Michael asked, "Was it a silver bullet? Is that why it had to be out to heal?"

Xander replied, "Yes, a regular bullet, she would've been able to expel it herself. She's lucky it wasn't a heart shot. You saw what that did to Alexis. It would have killed her instantly."

Casey was completely healed by the time Temple and Ivey got there. The only remanence of her being shot was her bloody shirt. Xander and Fitz filled them in on what happened while they waited for Casey to wake up.

Chapter Thirty-Nine

Ivey wanted so badly to go by her side but didn't dare, with Michael or Markus in the room. He stayed on the other side of the room by the front door.

Casey's eyes fluttered open and she started to wake up.

Michael smiled at her when her eyes fully opened and softly said, "You scared the shit out of us babe. You may not like it but you're not ever going out of this house again, without one of us with you."

Casey sat up with help from Angel. She rolled her right shoulder to the front and then to the back. It was a little sore but nothing like the pain she felt earlier. She smiled at Michael and while she took her hand to feel where the bullet hole use to be, she said, "I have no problem with that." She paused, looked at Ivey and replied, "Jake you might want to sit down for what I have to say."

Jake walked over and sat in the chair that was next to Casey, who was still sitting on the couch.

She let out a big sigh and said, "What I'm about to say to you, to both of you," she looked at Temple. "The first part you need to keep to yourselves."

Temple and Jake nodded yes.

Casey continued, "I turned into a wolf last night."

Jake and Temple's face showed surprise but they didn't say a word.

"I went looking for Markus and Angel and was tired after my run. I couldn't find them so I stopped to rest. When I got up awhile later, a car came down the road so I hid. Another car showed up a few minutes later and a guy got out of each vehicle. It was Paul and Alan."

Jake shifted in his chair.

Casey looked at him and replied, "I realize now he was the one you were protecting me from."

Jake smiled and looked down.

Casey scooted closer to him but addressed the whole group when she said, "I listened to their conversation. They admitted they trashed the bar and tried to blame Jake for it. You were right to take me into the station that night, they were going to do something to me. Paul was Sidney's boyfriend ... they think I had a part in Sidney's disappearance and there pissed at Jake for protecting me." She looked at Jake and said, "He knows you're onto him and wants us dead." Casey paused and started tearing up knowing the next thing she had to tell him. She hesitated but continued, "Jake, what I'm about to say, it's not going to be easy for you to hear." She paused, took a deep breath and said, "I heard them admit to killing Ariel."

Jake was in shock. He sat there staring at Casey, not saying a word, trying to comprehend what she had just told him.

Casey looked around and saw confused faces and said, "Ariel was his wife."

After Casey's explanation, Jake snapped. He put his head in his hands and became over wrought with emotion, as he rocked back and forth.

Casey slid down on the floor in front of him and hugged him.

He cried on her shoulder and as a tear fell down her cheek she said, "At least now you know for sure who did it and can get closure."

Michael was very uncomfortable with how close Ivey and Casey had become, behind his back. He couldn't hold his anger anymore and blurted out, "What the hell is this Casey?"

Casey turned around with a quickness and an angry expression, glaring at Michael.

He kept yelling, "How long has this been going on? When did you two get so buddy-buddy?"

Casey stood up and charged over to Michael yelling, "This is not the time or place Michael. He just found out who killed his wife ..."

Michael interrupted, "That's another thing. How did you know about his wife?"

Before Casey could answer, she felt light headed and stumbled backwards.

Fitz saw what was happening and yelled, "Michael get back," as he ran over and stood in between Casey and Michael.

Casey fell to the floor and went into fetal position.

Fitz continued, "She's shifting, guess we know anger is her trigger, for whatever she turns into."

Michael backed up and whispered, "I didn't mean ..."

No body acknowledged what he said because they were watching Casey.

Although it looked painful, Casey didn't make a sound. Her arms and legs started shrinking and her body started growing white fur. When the transformation was complete, lying where Casey had once lain was a White Bengal tiger. Casey got up on all fours and shook her whole body.

Michael tried to walk over to her and Fitz stopped him. "Remember, the first moments after the change, she'll only have animal instinct. Give her a minute."

Michael made a movement that caught Casey's attention and she hissed. The sound stopped Michael in his tracks.

Fitz planted his legs because he figured she was going to charge by her body language, and he was right.

She lunged but Fitz blocked her. She hissed at him and then rubbed up against him, purring.

Suddenly Xander yelled, "Casey don't do it."

Everyone was confused and what happened next only super naturals in the room felt.

Casey's power exploded out of her towards Fitz and Xander, making them hit the floor. The next thing everyone saw was Fitz in Tiger form and Xander as a big solid Black Wolf.

Casey sauntered over to Jake and rubbed up against him. She turned, looked at Fitz and Xander and thought, '*That's what you get for stopping me from getting to him.*'

Michael replied out loud, "I can hear you Casey."

'*Shut the fuck up Michael. Don't be here when I get back.*' She turned and bounded out the door.

After a look from Xander, Fitz took off after her.

Jake was still in shock with everything going on. He could only mutter, "We're just friends."

The statement pissed Michael off more and he jumped towards Ivey.

Xander moved in front of Michael.

Michael gritted his teeth and snapped, "You too, fuck this I'm leaving. I'm not staying in the house with him." Michael grabbed his keys and as he walked out the door, Angel pushed Markus and said, "Go with him, keep him out of trouble."

Markus gave her a quick kiss and jogged after Michael.

Chapter Forty

Casey was so pissed at Michael while running through the woods, she had no idea Fitz was right behind her.

They jumped over a road and then Fitz lunged at her from behind and knocked her feet out from under her, to get her to stop.

She hissed at him.

'Casey I'm sorry but I needed you to stop so we could talk.'

'What the hell? How can I hear you in this form?'

'You're my pack leader, pack members communicate by thought in animal form. You just have to form the bond, which we did when you forced Xander and I to shift.'

Casey got up and shook, *'I'm sorry about that, I was so mad. I wanted to lash out at Michael but was stopped, so I lashed out at the person that stopped me. You know you could have just yelled my name.'*

'Didn't think of that. I know your mad at me, but you would've never forgiven yourself if you had hurt him. You love him.'

'I know, you're right. He can get to me sometimes, though. Especially about Jake.'

'Ya'll should have told us what was going on.'

'Jake and I didn't know who to trust. We couldn't tell the police and didn't want ya'll to take matters in your own hands. Which is what you, Xander, Markus and especially Michael would've done.'

'That's probably true, however, Jeremy has a level head. He could've done something.'

'Hind sight is twenty-twenty Fitz.'

'When did you and Jake become close?'

'In North Carolina, he told me I was in danger but not who was after me. He told me about losing his wife ... and well ... we bonded.'

'I understand why you kept it from Michael, with his reaction.'

'I just wish he understood.'

'Yeah, that would make things easier. Let's head back home, hopefully everything has calmed down.'

'Home, huh.'

As they walked across the road Fitz continued, 'If you don't mind. Xander and I talked earlier about me staying up here to watch over you and try to keep you out of trouble.'

Before Casey could answer, she realized where they were and heard cars coming down the road. They both jumped over a log and hid.

Casey was having Deja vu.

Paul and Alan got out of their cars and Alan said, "I found out something."

Paul replied, "What?"

"My girlfriend, Tia, told me Casey shifted into a wolf last night. Hey, you don't think that's what you shot last night, do you?"

"I don't know," Paul pulled something out of his pocket. "But with these, it's not going to matter."

"What are they?"

"They're wolf bane silver bullets. It won't matter if I hit her heart. The wolf bane is poison to wolves."

They both laughed.

Casey was getting ready to lunge at them and Fitz stopped her.

Alan cleared his throat and said, "When are we going to kill Casey and Ivey?"

"Tonight, they won't be expecting us after the full moon. Where Casey will be, Ivey won't be too far away. If anyone else gets hit, then there just collateral damage."

Paul put his gun back in the holster after putting the new bullets in, turned to face the car and showed Alan the plan.

Casey yelled at Fitz, '*Can we kill them now?*'

'*You get Paul, I'll get the other guy.*'

Casey and Fitz jumped out of the woods and stalked up behind them. They were about two feet away when Casey let out a hiss.

Paul and Alan jumped around but it was too late.

Casey lunged and knocked Paul back onto the hood of the car and stood on her hind legs, leaning over him.

Alan ran and Fitz gave chase.

Casey was growling in Paul's face when she heard a gun go off. She looked down and knocked it out of his hand and went for his throat. She wrapped her glistening, white jagged teeth around his neck and bit down. She heard crunching and a snap. She pulled back with his throat in her teeth and his blood dripping out of her mouth.

There was no more movement from Paul.

She jumped down from what was left of Paul as Fitz came back. He saw her spit out his throat on the ground and lick her lips. Casey looked like she was going on pure animal instinct.

He stopped when he saw her and thought, *'Casey, are you ok?'*

'I'm not sorry at all.'

Fitz ran over to her as she stumbled, *'That's not what I meant, you were shot. Let's get you home, if you can shift back that would help. You forced us to shift, so when you shift back, Xander and I both do too.'*

Casey passed out trying to shift.

Fitz threw her over his back and tried to run as fast as he could, without dropping her. Halfway home he fell and Casey hit the ground with a thud.

The force of the fall made them shift back to human form and he ran all the way home with her in his arms.

Chapter Forty-One

Fitz barreled through the door holding Casey and startled everyone in the house.

Xander had turned back to human form as well and yelled, "What the hell happened now?"

Fitz was out of breath as he put her on the couch and said, "She was shot again, by the same guys from last night."

Temple jumped up and yelled, "Son of a bitch! I'm going to kill those two!"

Fitz was catching his breath when he said, "No need." He paused. "We can't get in trouble for anything we do in animal form, correct?"

Temple hesitantly replied, "No, just looks like an animal attack. Why?"

Fitz replied, "Let's just say, we won't ever have to worry about Paul or Alan again. Also, you might want to accidently come across an animal attack, about a mile east from here, before someone else does. It was on a dirt road."

Temple let out a big sigh and said, "Jake, you stay here and help. I'll go check out the scene. If it comes out that Paul and Alan were after you and Casey, I don't want to have to explain why you helped me find the scene of their death." He turned and walked out of the house and drove east.

Angel ran to call Markus and Michael.

Jake went to sit on the floor by Casey and held her hand.

Xander went to get what they would need to get the bullet out.

Fitz walked into the kitchen to clean Casey's blood off his hands.

Xander walked back in with the supplies and set up everything. He was getting ready to start when Fitz came out of the kitchen and yelled, "Stop!"

Xander jumped, froze and exclaimed, "What! What am I doing wrong?"

"Nothing, Paul used a new kind of bullet. It's a sliver bullet infused with wolf bane."

Xander looked at Ivey and handed him the tweezers. "You're the only one that can do this. It would kill or poison us and the bullet needs to come out now."

Jake slid up on his knees beside Casey, took the tweezers from Xander and started feeling for the bullet.

Michael and Markus ran in as he was pulling the bullet out and put it on the coffee table.

Michael screamed, "Get the hell away from her."

Jake fell backwards away from Michael, while Fitz jumped in between them and yelled, "He just saved her life, have some gratitude."

Michael stepped back from Fitz, as a look of terror filled his face.

Fitz continued, "The bullet had wolf bane in it. It's poisonous for all shifters but deadly to wolves, no matter what you do. She didn't die instantly because she wasn't in wolf form when she was shot. Jake got the bullet out quickly, so she's only feeling the effects of the poison ... for now. We need to get the antidote soon though, or she'll die."

Jake stood up slowly and replied, "I can help with that. I overheard that these bullets existed, so I researched what cured the poison. I actually have some in my car."

Everyone moved out of his way and he ran outside to get it.

Michael walked over and knelt by Casey. He looked at the gunshot wound, moved her hair from her face and asked, "Why does she have blood around her mouth?"

Jake was coming through the door with a small case when Fitz answered, "Because she ripped Paul's throat out."

Jake gasped, Michael was silent, Angel was in shock, Xander shook his head side to side but it was Markus who broke the silence when he said, "Wow, our girl is growing up. Second person she's killed in a month."

Angel smacked him on his upper arm.

Jake cleared his throat and walked over to Casey. He opened the box and brought out a prefilled vial of the antidote. He looked around at everyone and said, "This hasn't been tested, I don't know if this will work."

Everyone looked towards Michael and he said, "We have to try something. If we don't she'll die."

Jake took the top off the needle and administered the shot. He stood up, looked around the room and said, "Now, it's a waiting game."

Chapter Forty-Two

Angel brought in a pan of water and started cleaning the blood from Casey's lifeless body.

In the meantime, the guys went outside to talk.

Fitz started the conversation, "Casey and I talked before she was injured. Michael, you really need to come to grips for Casey, that her and Jake are friends. They made a connection from both losing a spouse, it's something people can bond over. Plus, now that we know her trigger for her tiger is anger, you really don't want to piss her off. At least until she can control it."

Michael turned to Jake, started to say something and stopped. He turned back to Fitz and said, "She's been angry before and she hadn't turned. What was so different today?"

Xander answered, "Her wolf form is the dominate shifter since she received it from scratches, not a serum. When she shifted last night, that opened the door for both forms of her animals to be released. When she learns to control it, she'll be able to become either one she wants."

Markus tapped him on his shoulder and nodded towards Jake.

Michael sighed and said, "Ivey, thank you for saving Casey's life. On that alone, I can forgive you and we can make a fresh start. Seems like you and Casey are friends, so I guess we'll be seeing you around more. I'm sorry for the way I acted. You care for her as a good friend and want to protect her, I realize that now. She needs all the protection she can get, are we good?"

Jake smiled and said, "Yes, on one condition."

Michael hesitantly asked, "What?"

"You call me Jake."

Michael laughed and replied, "Don't push it."

They shook each other's hands and were laughing when Angel stuck her head out of the door. "She's waking up fella's."

Michael of course was the first through the door.

Casey was sitting up in the middle of the couch.

He went over, sat by her and held her hand.

Jake came in right afterward, Xander, Markus and Fitz were right behind him.

Casey looked up at Jake and smiled.

Jake started to walk over to her but stopped and looked at Michael.

Michael gave him a nod, so Jake finished his walk and sat down by Casey.

She took his hand in hers.

Jake looked at Michael and he shrugged. Jake relaxed and looked at Casey.

She still had the smile on her face when she said, "I heard you pulled the bullet out and had the antidote that saved my life. Thank you, Jake."

"Your welcome."

She held up Michael and Jake's hand and shook them. "Maybe now things will be better between you two."

Michael smiled, kissed the back of her hand and replied, "We've already come to an agreement, we're good."

"Wow, I really missed a lot, huh? Maybe I should get shot more often." Casey laughed but no one else did. She started to get up but both Jake and Michael stopped her. "I'm ok guys. I would really like to take a shower."

Xander stepped up and helped her up. He gave her a hug and said, "Since you're better and the threat has been eliminated, I'm going to head back to North Carolina and check out Tia."

Casey raised an eyebrow and he continued, "Fitz told me what ya'll heard."

"I understand. Be careful, we don't know what she's up too. Drive safe."

"I will ... oh ... it's ok if Fitz stays right."

"Oh yeah, he can have one of the rooms upstairs."

Michael smiled at Fitz and patted his shoulder. "Glad to have the extra enforcer."

Xander finished hugging Casey, said byes to everyone else and walked out the door.

Angel walked over to Casey after Xander finished hugging her and helped her to her to the bathroom.

CHAPTER FORTY-THREE

Casey leaned against the counter for stability while Angel started the water.

She walked out into the bedroom to get Casey clothes for after her shower.

Casey gripped the countertop because the room started spinning, her eyes rolled into the back of her head and she slid down the countertop, to the floor.

Angel heard the thump and ran into the bathroom. When she saw Casey unconscious on the floor, she yelled for help.

Fitz and Michael sprinted into the room and saw what was happening. Fitz got the bed ready while Michael picked her up and laid her in the bed. Michael covered her up, as Fitz felt her forehead and replied, "She's burning up."

Michael walked to the doorway and yelled, "Jake get in here and bring the bullet." Michael looked at Fitz and he asked, "Your sense of smell is strong, right?"

Fitz nodded.

"I need you to smell the bullet ... see if we missed something."

"I can't touch it."

"I know, Jake is going to hold it for you."

Jake walked in as Michael said that and walked over to Fitz.

He smelled it, flinched backwards and replied, "That's a high quantity of concentrated wolf bane. Jake, do you have another dose of antidote?"

"Yes, I brought all of it in." Jake went to grab the case and put the bullet back in the living room. He interrupted Markus consoling Angel, while she was telling Jeremy what happened.

Michael walked over and sat on the bed by Casey. It pained him to see her like this.

Jake walked back to the room with the case in the opposite hand he had held the bullet in. He handed it to Michael and said, "I shouldn't touch the shot or Casey because of holding the bullet."

Michael and Fitz agreed and Jake went to wash his hands.

Michael opened the case, saw no more pre-made vials and closed it back to wait for Jake, because neither him or Fitz knew how much antidote to give her.

Jake came back in the room and sat on the other side of Casey on the bed.

Michael handed him the case.

He opened it, took out a syringe and vial of liquid. He pressed the needle in the top, pulled the plunger to the level needed and then put the vial back in the case. He flipped the syringe upside down, flicked it with his finger and pushed the plunger until liquid came out, so there were no air bubbles. He stuck the needle in her arm and pushed down on the plunger.

Once he was done he looked at Fitz and Michael and said, "Now, we wait to see if she needs another dose."

Michael laid on one side of Casey and Fitz laid on the other.

Jake sat in the chair in the corner of the room, watching them lay beside her, wishing it was him. He kept taking her temperature throughout the night and it finally broke at three in the morning.

Fitz got up to go stretch and take over watch for Markus and Angel, so they could get some sleep.

Jake walked over and sat down where Fitz had been. He grabbed the rag in the bowl beside the bed, rung it out and patted Casey's forehead.

Her eyes started to flutter open.

Once they were completely opened, she smiled at Jake and reached for his hand. She took Michael's hand in her other one and fell back asleep.

Michael woke up, saw what happened and chuckled when he saw the look on Jake's face. He softly replied, "It's ok Jake, she apparently needs you. I don't like sharing but it's what Casey wants, so I'll have to be ok with it." He paused. "I would make yourself comfortable. I can hear her relaxing more with both of us here."

Chapter Forty-Four

Several hours later, Jake and Michael were awoken by Fitz and Agent Temple, entering the bedroom.

Casey had been awake for twenty minutes or so, enjoying the quiet and Michael's and Jake's company. Her smile dissipated when she saw the look of concern on Temple and Fitz's faces. She scooted up in the bed and hesitantly asked, "What's wrong?"

Temple replied, "There's no easy way to say this ... there were no bodies or trace of anything that Fitz described, on the road he sent me too. I even checked other roads around the area, that's what took me so long to get back."

Michael sat up and asked, "What could that mean?"

Temple replied, "It could mean that Paul and Alan were working for someone else. The scene was completely cleaned, not even tire tracks. This was a professional clean-up job."

Jake sat up this time and said, "This means the threat to Casey and myself is still out there."

Temple nodded. "I believe so."

Before anyone could comment, Michael said, "Well then, it makes sense that we all be under one roof, to protect each other."

Everyone looked at Michael surprisingly and Casey put her hand on his and said, "Thank you."

Michael replied, "It's the right thing to do. They're after him for protecting you. He saved your life, I owe him." He looked at Jake and asked, "Is that ok with you?"

Jake still not knowing how to take this 'new' Michael simply nodded yes.

Michael continued, "We'll go get some of your stuff later. You can stay upstairs, in the extra room by Fitz."

Casey smiled at them both as Jake felt her forehead.

He said, "Your temperature is gone and you look so much better. You gave us a scare last night, had to give you a second dose of the antidote."

Casey replied, "I do feel a lot better, still a little tired though. I'm going to go back to sleep."

Fitz walked over and kissed Casey on the forehead. She flinched and played it off. "Your lips are cold." He smiled.

Michael and Jake let go of Casey's hands, got up and Fitz and Temple followed them into the living room.

Temple said, "Sounds like ya'll have things taken care of here. Jake, I'm giving you time off until it's safe. Just remember everyone, the threat is still out there so keep your eyes open."

Everyone nodded in agreement and he left.

The guys went into the kitchen to make plans for Casey and Jake's safety.

Chapter Forty-Five

Once Casey was alone, she snuggled back under the covers and repeated the vision over and over in her head she had when Fitz kissed her. She played it off because she wasn't sure what she had seen, was a threat and didn't want to worry the guys.

In her vision, she saw three teenagers standing in the bar, two males and one female. One male had brown hair, the other black and the female had fiery red hair; they didn't look like anyone she had met before but she felt a closeness to them.

She wondered if the vision had something to do with her holding Michael and Jake's hand, at the same time Fitz kissed her forehead. She didn't understand why the three strangers would have such an impact on her and it didn't explain why she felt love towards them.

A love that grew every time she replayed back the vision in her head.